An Appropriate Place

a novel

Lise Bissonnette

Translated by
Sheila Fischman

ANANSI

First published as *Un Lieu Approprié* in 2001 by Les Éditions du Boréal

Published in 2002 by
House of Anansi Press Inc.
110 Spadina Ave., Suite 801
Toronto, ON, M5V 2K4
Tel. 416-363-4343
Fax 416-363-1017
www.anansi.ca

Distributed in Canada by
Publishers Group Canada
250A Carlton Street
Toronto, ON, M5A 2L1
Tel. 416-934-9900
Toll free order numbers:
Tel. 800-663-5714
Fax 800-565-3770

06 05 04 03 02   1 2 3 4 5

NATIONAL LIBRARY OF CANADA CATALOGUING IN PUBLICATION

Bissonnette, Lise
[Lieu approprié English]
An appropriate place / Lise Bissonnette. -- 1st ed.

Translation of: Un lieu approprié.
ISBN 0-88784-680-7

I. Title. II. Title: Lieu approprié English.

PS8553.I877288L5313 2002   C843'.54   C2002-904129-5
PQ3919.2.B52L5413 2002

Canada Council **Conseil des Arts**
for the Arts **du Canada**

*We acknowledge for their financial support of our publishing program the Canada Coun-
cil for the Arts, the Ontario Arts Council, and the Government of Canada through the
Book Publishing Industry Development Program (BPIDP). This book was made possible
in part through the Canada Council's Translation Grants Program.*

for Godefroy-M. Cardinal

ONE

AT THE VERY MOMENT when Gabrielle Perron is brushing against her chauffeur's knee, he slams on the brakes. For the last time. The limousine comes to a halt across the pavement, the door slams and, instead of going to open Gabrielle's, Jean-Charles becomes absorbed in a bed of begonias, a pallid spot on the already yellow lawns on rue des Bouleaux where a single eponymous birch tree is growing, sickly.

Gabrielle joins him just as he turns away, she sees the little calico cat whose brains are spreading onto the white begonias, its forehead split down the middle and its life departing through an orange smudge, its black-and-grey flecked belly stops twitching, the eyes are already closed. Gabrielle grazes the sweating muzzle — she who detests being kissed by a cat — but she has to put off her caress till later.

And so all is well, despite the incident. Jean-Charles is dropping her off one last time at 10,005 rue des Bouleaux; it was a mistake for her to sit in the front, but the backseat was jammed with the thousand items left over when an office is cleared out — the papers, the photos under glass, the collection of prints by Charlène Lemire that she'd been one of the first to admire and that now, in her home, would finally be given the softer light necessary for their silken ghosts. There was also, wrapped in old-maidish tartan, the huge and fragile rosewood ashtray that had belonged to a prewar premier and that the museum didn't want, nor did the custodian of the storerooms in Parliament, where smoking was now forbidden. But Gabrielle Perron had sat in front today to be silent in the presence of the man to the nape of whose neck she'd been speaking for four years, his name is Jean-Charles and he has never wavered, neither when avoiding a deer in the pitch black night nor while driving through a demonstration in broad daylight.

All is well, he will empty out the limousine and go on his way, he will always believe that she brushed against his knee to draw his attention to the animal, she'll offer him a glass of water at the kitchen counter and walk him to the fourth-floor elevator, he won't imagine that she would have stripped naked today, in front of his brown eyes and his firm hand, in a puddle of sunlight from the living room to which he couldn't imagine being admitted.

Jean-Charles has wadded a page of a newspaper lying on the backseat, he wipes the bumpers of the navy Chevrolet, such a small cat can't have left any traces. Gabrielle wonders if he too is trying to put on a brave face, but apparently not. "We'll have to find out who the cat belongs to," he says. She disagrees, rue des Bouleaux is lined with identical apartment buildings, all pink bricks and deserted white balconies, very few children there have cats, Gabrielle knows that, for she bought the apartment because there weren't many children and she'd thought that animals were not allowed. Instead, she sends Jean-Charles to the concierge, who will know how to dispose of the animal and restore the line of begonias. "Her name is Fatima," says Gabrielle.

Plump and hefty, she is already on the doorstep, a still-young woman whom Gabrielle pictures always sitting at a table over hams and potatoes. Between her legs stands a little girl Gabrielle has never seen, but then, what does she actually know about Fatima? The building is new, the hallways shiny, the garbage cans taken out on time, there's no need for conversation.

The child cries over her little calico cat, she swallows, then she howls, then she shrieks the tears from her throat.

Her hair is too short, her eyes are too huge, she could be an embryonic seamstress in a factory, she'll know how to blaspheme before she reaches puberty. Like Fatima, who is shouting now in her own language, guttural, a language of the sun but of curses too, of which Gabrielle knows that she herself is the object. Rue des Bouleaux murmurs now like the lanes of her childhood, when the mothers cursed one another between the clotheslines and the boys deliberately killed all the cats, in the sheds at night.

Jean-Charles has two sons, Jean and Charles, teenagers who perhaps do the same in their part of town with its still-lively laneways. Gabrielle sighs. She wonders in what way the brain of a cat is less than that of a child, on the brink of summer on rue des Bouleaux, in Laval.

She offers an apology that isn't heard, goes back and forth with Jean-Charles from the limousine to the fourth floor, while Fatima finally drops the little corpse into a garbage bag. The chauffeur will be entitled to a glass of water. From the vestibule he won't be able to see the puddle of sunlight in the living room that Gabrielle Perron will air out. Finally now, in June, she is going home to the place where she told her life to wait for her.

There are three things to do to make the place liveable. Disconnect the answering machine so that unknown supplicants, hearing only a ring, will henceforth apply elsewhere. Buy flowers, potting soil and flower boxes to dress up the balcony, because now she'll be there to water them. She'd like too some ivy that would climb up a trellis on the east side, where the vacant lot was supposed to be turned into a park but where, instead, small houses for small growing families had sprouted, happy owners of garden furniture behind tall fences. But first she'll have to learn how to grow ivy, which needs to take root somewhere. And she must arrange the books on the shelves she'd made to measure for the guest room, with a sliding ladder for looking at books near the ceiling, the idea comes from castles. Large sections of shelves are still empty, for five years she has shelved only novels, art books and the works of sociology and politics that she had underlined and thought she'd understood in Strasbourg or Paris, that she'd brought home so proudly in her student trunk. There was a metre of Rosa Luxemburg, by Rosa the Red herself or by others, half that by Enver Hoxha, a very incomplete collection of *Esprit* above the complete collection of *Parti pris* and then, in alphabetical order, the material for her thesis on palingenesis. At one glance, she can identify the books that mattered from their spines: Madaule, locked inside his Christianity, Poulantzas, who killed himself and Touraine, who still today talks about the change of which she'd thought she would be the transmitter over the course of a summer like this one, locked inside words while other brunettes were being married in white.

She'd had to reinforce the corners carefully so that the weight of her library wouldn't rest entirely on the floor, apartments in Laval don't have the joists that castles do. Now she will be able to put away the green papers and the white papers and the commission reports, the books on sovereignty and federalism, cases of them were delivered the previous week after being flung into boxes any old way in the big office that she left without regret. She'll have to go through them and preserve only those documents that she can recollect, that she cares about because she contributed paragraphs or chapters to them, or because she found in them echoes of her own developing social commitment. She'll get down to it tomorrow.

This afternoon she is still full of energy. The refrigerator is empty, she'll have to get bread, milk, salmon from the fish store that's opened in the mall adjacent to the highway, and maybe get some *choux à la crème*, if she has any, from Irène, the woman who has given her own name to her white cakes. Then she'll just have to put some Sauternes on ice, and at seven o'clock, when the sun won't set on her balcony because it gives onto the northern side of the Rivière des Prairies, though you can see its light dying over Montreal and its lives, for which she is no longer responsible, she will finally begin to resemble Colette, the photo of Colette at her window looking onto the garden of the Palais-Royal, surrounded by faded books, adrift in her memories of lovers, and tasting the sugar as the aroma of the last coffee wafts up.

Gabrielle Perron has no wrinkles, but she wants the time to see them come; this summer will be perfect. Sitting on the counter is the Sico paint card, she picked it up at the hardware store months before, thinking that she would repaint the whites, they're turning grey in the kitchen and the living room, the finishing is downscale in these apartments that were hastily put up as soon as the zoning laws permitted. It will be white again, because of the paintings, which don't tolerate colours, neither pale nor bright, but there are plenty of whites on a Sico card, matte ones and glossy ones, ivories and velvets, orchid and lily, Adriatic stones and Abitibi snow. Above all, she wants nothing iridescent.

She'll have to call Madeleine, but not today, even if she would enjoy hearing her prattle away, over light wine, about the disarray of her latest encounter — a man she met in the supermarket or at the university — whom she'll have undressed and dressed again between midnight and dawn if he wasn't married, to whom she'll have neglected to give her phone number. The last one was from Cambodia and he'd been one of the rare ones who knew how to disappear discreetly, Madeleine had even been slightly put out. In any event, on a sunny day like this she'd be at the pool, colouring herself amber. She'll try to talk Gabrielle out of white, she herself never wears it, it's hard on the complexion of any woman over forty.

Gabrielle Perron's Toyota, a cream one, will be cool in the underground parking space. Not a sound from the corridor, that's another reason why she chose to live here, with walls and an elevator so blind that you only encounter the shadows of neighbours there, they sometimes say "hello" or "have a nice day," like characters on American television, and if they know who Gabrielle Perron is, which she doubts, they behave as if she is merely the owner of apartment 401, with a balcony like theirs, and otherwise of no interest.

She goes to pick up her mail on the left side of the lobby. Virtually nothing — a leaflet from a real estate agent, but Gabrielle has no interest in selling, and an invitation to a benefit dinner for the party, which she's no longer obliged to attend. It's nice to be able to tear them to pieces.

To be done: order paint, ivory or off-white as the clerk says, and Gabrielle pictures millions of pigments just off the scale, prettily, around her enormous windows, then bread, milk and finally salmon. There are no *choux à la crème* at Irène's. She'll have to go directly home, she's always afraid of poisoning herself with stale fish, even though they assure her that the crushed ice in the display cases keeps it cool, it comes mainly from the Pacific, thousands of kilometres in refrigerated trucks and who knows how many hours in the open, in those little fish stores that are always run by boys with dark hands. What she likes about salmon, what restores her confidence, is the pink colour that in a few moments will burn under the broiler, a dish for a woman on her own who is elegant enough to be in tune with the dusk, so many would gobble a piece of cheese in front of the TV set and mope around, waiting for night.

As she leaves the parking lot, she sees that some teenagers have put up a booth with a large banner warning of a new famine in Ethiopia. She'd thought the disaster was over, but you never know with desertification and global warming and the forgotten people whose lives are no more stable than bubbles, the real story never makes it to our newspapers. Now, at the onset of a heat wave, the young people are selling polar bears decked out in red tuques, scarves and mittens, mounds of them sit in big cartons, they recycle unsold Christmas stock from Eaton's, salve your conscience for twenty dollars a shot. Gabrielle ends up with a stuffed animal on the passenger seat, the timing is good, she'll make a gift of it to Fatima's daughter who is her Ethiopia today, her little devastated zone in the sun.

Fatima always answers right away, as if she spends her life on the doorstep, her concierge's apartment is tiny, you can see the ironing board jutting out from the kitchenette into the crowded living room, where a huge aquarium fills the entire wall on the right, to each his library. The child is in front of the TV set, where a half-naked woman is crackling under the bullets of an invisible killer. Her eyes, which were weeping a while ago at the gentle convulsions of a calico cat, are scathing. The stuffed animal won't do. Gabrielle holds it out instead to Fatima, who is again displaying the closed smile that she's noted for, it's part of her job description. Gabrielle hasn't earned even a hint of forgiveness, but at least the day is slipping past a forgettable misfortune. The garbage truck will be here at six a.m. and, after all, she couldn't offer the little girl another cat, that would have been despicable; anyway it takes time to get over the death of a cat, at least according to Madeleine, who's had several and who claims that it's harder to recover from being abandoned by a cat than by a lover.

Fatima arranges the toy with its back to the aquarium, on the armrest of a flowered easy chair, and the mood does lighten. To connect with it, Gabrielle talks about painting. Does she know of a painter in the vicinity? One with satisfied customers in the building? It's not urgent, but Gabrielle has been away so much in recent years, she's not sure where to inquire. Fatima has an accent that sounds at once Spanish and German, at least to Gabrielle, who knows nothing but a few sounds of the so-distant Alsace. No, she wouldn't dare to recommend anyone, but there's a boy in 202 who did quite a few odd jobs for the owner of 404, the terrace apartment, last month. The man seemed pleased, he'd even let the boy have the key for the day, as long as he returned it to Fatima at five o'clock. And that's how a concierge knows everything and nothing.

Gabrielle has occasionally run into the shadow who lives in 404, with a view of the sunset but also of the row of apartments opposite, all the way to the highway ramp, on rue des Mélèzes, rue des Érables, rue des Lilas, rue des Amélanchiers, though none of these trees grows in Laval. He's old, he wears thick glasses of a kind that opticians don't sell any more, he looks like an activist in her party who kept pondering the same books, though at least he could quote them in timely fashion to young people devoid of memory, which was reassuring. She'll ask him about the boy. It will all work out, the eyes of Fatima's daughter are still just as scathing, but they're focussed now on a commercial for La Ronde and its water slides. Timidly, Gabrielle finally dares to ask her name. "Virginia," Fatima replies. Virginia is the daughter of a remote cousin, now American, who shipped her here for the summer. Actually, Gabrielle had been under the impression that Fatima didn't have a husband and therefore, most likely, no daughter.

The fourth floor has the disadvantage of being the top one; in return for its guaranteed silence, there is the summer dampness, which comes in through the insulation in the roof. Someday she'll have to replace the beautiful neutral grey carpeting, which is starting to fade despite the museum-quality sheers that she's hung on the windows to protect her paintings and the original colours of the big and very costly antique armoire that had travelled via an Outremont antique dealer from a seigneury to an apartment in Laval. She should have insisted on oak floors, but the carpet was included in the price of the apartment, she hadn't anticipated the musty smell that was trapped there in winter and did not disappear altogether in the spring. There are decorators nowadays who are bringing back a kind of linoleum with a permanently waxed finish on which to lay Oriental carpets woven of strong silk that won't wear out. That's something she'll have to look into.

Finally, into a tall glass Gabrielle pours Pernod and orange juice, drops in ice cubes one by one. She has never developed a liking for the liquorice taste, first experienced in France. But it's what you drink in the summer when you finally settle into a white wicker chair with an apple green cushion, looking out on the Rivière des Prairies at the testosterone-powered boats. At least from here she can't hear the roaring made by men who wouldn't dare to live by themselves in a fourth-floor apartment in Laval, who'd think they were surrounded and would break things to prove otherwise.

For her, so sure of herself, this is an appropriate place. A honeycomb cell where Gabrielle can finally experience the "after." She sips her drink. She contemplates putting on music, the posthumous *Nocturne* by Heinrich Wilhelm

Ernst, played by Midori at Carnegie Hall, one of the few discoveries made through her membership, now expired, in the Columbia Record Club. But if she did that, at the beginning of this evening that's so bare, in her mind's eye she would see the slender image of a foreign woman straining over her strings, and the crowd at the concert. And there would be noise.

The ice cubes dissolve, the water dulls the accents of orange and liquorice, the caned chair back scrapes the shoulders of Gabrielle Perron, who thought that she was capable of existing amid silence.

She has nothing to think about. Nothing. A very beautiful spider, pitch black, clings to the railing, apparently without a web. Five more hours till midnight. She really should have some ivy on the eastern exposure and, in the flower boxes, red geraniums. She has always been able to think about something, but never about meaningless things like Jean-Charles's knee or the oozing brains of a calico cat. She gets up to open a tin of white asparagus and the new bottle of cold-pressed, extra virgin olive oil, uncork the Sauternes, light the broiler. She'll see tomorrow. The salmon steak — it's perfectly normal in this heat, which is definitely outrageous — tastes slightly off. It's just as well that there were no *choux à la crème*, they'd have gone bad.

TWO

A MONTH LATER, Pierre has brought the place under his control. He has transported gallons of paint, bought brushes and rollers, piled and protected the furniture in the middle of the living room. His dexterity is remarkable in a boy his age, who's not supposed to know how to work. He has respected Gabrielle's silence on the days when she was listing her entire library on computer, he even helped her modify the program to add cross-references.

Outside, there's a drought. The river will become a prairie, Gabrielle predicts, when they meet on the balcony at noon, where he has helped her put up an awning. She prepares lentil salad, cold pasta with clams, roasted peppers, sugared raspberries. He joins her in drinking light sangria. They had very little to say to each another until the day when he began to show an interest in her paintings.

First, in the retriever portrayed by Anne Ashton between two rosebushes, a dog indifferent to the hunt, posing on the tips of his long, arched legs, a print for the boudoir of a marquise. It wasn't modern art, he was surprised to note, claiming that he'd spotted some everywhere else in the apartment and that he preferred a beige and silent Gaucher, so brilliantly closed around its interior folds that it takes away your appetite for images. "What he's done is give a colour to a bad mood," said Pierre in the tone of a budding connoisseur, already a touch snide. Anne Ashton's dog provided an opportunity to put him in his place, to explain to him that Gaucher's terrible break with the living could be found just as well in the rendering of an animal from another century, whose artificially arched posture in a fake warren questioned any wish to paint reality, world without end, then and now. And had he not noticed the insect on a rose petal that didn't correspond to any known species? It would take a great deal of subtlety to grasp the new directions of art, the deceptive return to the anecdotal that seemed attractive, sometimes witty, but that always carried with it an impression of death.

He had to struggle to listen, no doubt because of his lack of vocabulary, and afterwards he avoided expressing an opinion on the works prematurely. Instead, he let his opinions fall as questions until he finally approached the most intimidating, the series of paintings in the corridor, near-frescoes that seemed to be formless beings intertwined, hairless and with heavy stomachs, neither men nor women, breasts wounded, sex gashed, lashing under a pale sky shot through with thorns. "Still, you could think that the painter used velvet brushes," he ventured to say. Gabrielle taught him that this expert, amorous series was the work of a young woman. Laurence Cardinal's line, shot through like the mind of a medium, had more to say about the gentleness and the cruelty of lovers than she would ever learn, though artists' loves are supremely tormented.

Pierre had become obsessed with these uninhibited canvases that seemed to move as he walked past them. And Gabrielle had been caught up in the game of educating him, to the point of mentioning without embarrassment the desire smouldering under the ashen grey of the faces, the shudder that flowed beneath the light brown of the thighs, the orgasm that cut the red, colour of blood and of sex, of the flesh — all that linked by a furious charcoal that had streaked the scenes as if they were the last ones.

"You can't know," she'd begun without thinking, in the middle of a leaden Friday. And now, because it was the logical next step, he wanted to know. As if he were inquiring about another painting, he had asked her to make love. Because the time had come, he said, and because girls his age paid no attention to him. Anyway, it was reciprocal, he preferred the company of older women, like his mother's friend who had taken him in for the summer and was now all wrapped up in her lover's recent death.

Gabrielle had given in without a fuss, perhaps a competitive spirit still inhabited her, she'd be a contrast with the weeping widow. Besides, she'd felt an urge for that particular game, belly and legs abruptly hot, it would be good on the floor, on rough sheets smelling of camphor already stained with ivory white, he could spill himself onto them without embarrassment because she'd throw them out afterwards, she had planned it.

Gabrielle brought their plates inside, turned off the air conditioner, joined Pierre in the shower to be at the beginning no more than a shadow, matte and brown, against his, pale and musky. It would be best to hide from him the creases under her breasts, at her knees, at the place where shoulder meets arm. She'd have hidden them even from a man of fifty, she wasn't one of those women who enjoys bites — the light is one. She rubbed him slowly, then soothed him while she guided his hand towards other creases, those that stay beautiful, that open and flow with her particular milk in the lavender-scented foam and the fingers of an overexcited boy. She pressed her sex at length against his thigh because later, in the living room, it would be too quick. He lay down awkwardly in fact, didn't know how to caress her in the open air, she'd teach him in the days to come. She guided him into her, and his slight movement before he collapsed created a flash in her belly, made her flow again, so wet. She was surprised and still hungry, she mustn't.

Madeleine would have recommended buying a vibrator

instead. After wearing out a good many overly young lovers, she had something against them all — youngsters who interfere with your life for months, who insult the rules of spelling in their love notes that take the form of praise of older women, and then one morning, with their bare eyes, look you up and down with contempt, leaving you more withered than you are. And that's without counting the sense of incest, which makes you come with guilt. But Gabrielle would say nothing to Madeleine, this one was going to be brief. It would be over when the painting was, and the apartment wasn't all that big.

Around three o'clock, after Pierre had left, she poured herself some ice water and savoured her new life, resigning herself to her recent folly. This child whom she'd teach about sex, everything she had sought and so rarely found, would be a mere rite of passage. He had the eyes of autumn, of a wolf, maybe, as in *Peter and the Wolf*, do you remember, Gabrielle, Prokofiev and the night?

Oh yes, she remembered, the first of the wolves.

There is winter and a girl of sixteen, neither very pretty nor very tall, and she's spending the weekend at her friend Guylaine's. They are studying piano, but they consider the lessons old-fashioned and prefer gatherings where you mix with boys and with ideas about resistance. That day, in Guylaine's enormous bedroom — she has rich parents and a house in the suburbs with a driveway so long that they need a snowblower — they are drawing up the bylaws of their student association, copying them from a model being used at the university, everything from obligatory dues to rules of meetings, from election regulations to the disciplinary committee. They have hopes of retaining the key elements when the time comes to adopt them. The nuns are leaving the veil one by one, only the last holdouts are still at the college, the chaplain preaches a secular moral code and the nuns don't dare to stop him from discussing democracy with girls who are, even so, not as rebellious as Marie-Claire Blais, whose novels are beginning to win praise.

Guylaine's mother has a maid who makes beds and does dishes, to Gabrielle her friend is a princess. Guylaine though is modest enough to serve her. For it's Gabrielle who knows everything, why to found associations, with whom to correspond to register for the national congress, how to start the fundraising by inviting a chansonnier, the shyest of them, the one who sings about the sea without grumbling, he won't cost too much. Gabrielle intends to dress all in black to meet his agent, she dares to laugh at the lace that fills her friend's bedroom, that trims the dressing table and the windows and the canopy bed. Guylaine doesn't defend herself well, except for the Icart prints, they're worth a lot of money, her father chose them, he's a connoisseur of everything. The father is a pharmacist, that's the only thing that is clear in Gabrielle's eyes, he doesn't say much, is lost in thought behind his cigarettes and his books, an avant-garde Christian, says his daughter. Gabrielle sees him as a kind of hermit, resigned to his women — wife, daughter, maid — in another life he'd have been a saint, he sighs constantly and goes to the art galleries by himself on Saturdays, where he unearths old works. He says that art is now deteriorating, and his daughter repeats it.

Gabrielle doubts that, because the new art appeals to her, but Guylaine's father is the sole authority she dares not take issue with, she'd be afraid of losing her friend, who is so gentle and who listens to everything with fervour. She envies her that father whose silence is so laden with thoughts, while her own father doesn't have a single one. He extricates himself from his eternal bus, the number 50, only to stumble through a moronic account of his day, then start again on the morrow. His schedule, the inspector, worn brakes, road maintenance, lost old ladies, bawling children, insolent students. He doesn't wonder if the world is deteriorating, he's not in it, his eyes shine only when he talks about an imminent move to Montréal-Nord where Italian builders are finally putting up houses a person can afford. Gabrielle will loathe Montréal-Nord.

On this Saturday night, as on all the others, the pharmacist goes down to the basement, an entresol fixed up according to his canons. They aren't his ancestors although they give that impression — the two portraits of anonymous dignitaries of Nouvelle-France that flank a rough antique buffet. By Jean-Baptiste Roy-Audy, according to the bronze plate on the jigsawed frame, a man in black with a collar so high he could have been a priest, and a woman in rusty green, her hair pulled back so tightly she must be the mother of priests. A rosary drips from her fingers, she prays eternally for the salvation of colonial souls. The buffet in fact has something of the sacristy about it, even the blue-fringed lamp was made from a ceremonial candlestick; antique dealers don't have to empty the churches, they're doing it themselves, for next to nothing. In the pharmacist's den the armchairs are wingbacks, he calls them *voltaires* but neither Guylaine nor Gabrielle is familiar with that name, the writer is not to be found in the convent library. As for the pharmacist's, it has rows of *Les semaines sociales du Canada*, bound by year, in the company of everything by Claudel, Péguy, Mauriac. But he considers them too young and too girlish to enter there, they have to play the piano while he reads Bernanos, *Les grands cimetières sous la lune*.

Which is what they are doing one Saturday before dinner, puzzling out a piece for four hands, grinding away at a rather out-of-tune Heintzman. Then Guylaine goes upstairs to look for her mother while Gabrielle plays from memory the piano version of *Peter and the Wolf*, whose phrasing, while childish, flows gravely towards the man reading. Long afterwards, she will ask herself if this moment hadn't been the first instance of the false innocence she'll learn to master, if by accentuating the melancholic effect of the wolf's notes she hadn't wanted to trouble the dry individual at her side. Why had she turned towards him before launching into the twittering of the bird unless it was to test the line she'd just held out? In a moment he'd been all over her, clinging to her back, hairy arms grasping her shoulders, hand seeking the buds of her breasts under the angora sweater, boring into her body to nestle it in his chest. She remembered the acid smell of his green-striped woollen necktie as much as the tongue that had scraped her neck, and the seconds to free herself and run away.

She should have cried out, but instead she had climbed the stairs, getting back her aplomb, she'd gone into the kitchen quite naturally, offering to help. She should have had her heart in her throat instead of feeling a shiver of pride at the person she'd become in this bourgeois house. That at least was the image of the moment she had finally settled on: that of a young girl who had been able to dominate at the first assault the droppings that ooze from Pharisees in heat. There had been so many others in what would be her profession that the pharmacist had been a useful preliminary exercise.

She was forgetting that, all the same, she had steered clear of Guylaine for days and that later she had constantly avoided the calm gaze of the father who seemed to have no reason to feel guilty. "Maybe he was just being affectionate, friendly," suggested Madeleine, who preferred the least awkward interpretations for anything having to do with sex. Maybe.

She had never breathed a word to Guylaine, who every now and then remained her friend. Guylaine had a beautiful soul. She'd enrolled in nursing science because her father pictured her in a lab coat, following in his tradition, but also because she had an image of herself relieving all forms of suffering, she dreamed of holding the hands of children with cancer and incontinent old people, in the same way that Gabrielle was waiting impatiently to enrol in sociology courses given by Guy Rocher, whose vocabulary was sprinkled through the communiqués from the *Presse étudiante nationale*. Social classes meant her at the bottom with Guylaine above, and equalization was in the wind, it was inevitable. It had seemed certain to her late one summer, next to the pool in the garden that suburbanites were beginning to take better care of, when Guylaine had confirmed that she was engaged to a nice accountant who'd been hovering for two years and who had just inherited, prematurely, a chain of book and stationery stores. Guylaine was well aware that boredom lay in wait after too many of her Fernand's embraces, she was not so dumb and she'd already sampled the body of this future golfer obsessed with performance. The books he sold did not include those Gabrielle was engrossed in and which she no longer even bothered to tell her friend about. Anyway, she'd moved on from Rocher to Bourdieu, whose more indignant jargon gave her an appetite for action. Guylaine would have been alarmed.

To get a glimpse of the future, she had only needed to catch the hint of concern in the eyes of her friend, who was going to get married and was well aware that she was choosing the wrong path, nearly apologizing. "It will be simple, in the country, the church will be a formality, my dress is ecru and short, the caterer will be waiting at the chalet in Saint-Sauveur, there'll be a little dancing, in October it will be too chilly to have the party outdoors. It will be perfectly ordinary, nothing fancy, you can come on your own if you want." Of course she would go on her own, to watch the assurance of the rich quietly fade away, to waltz out of step with the pharmacist whose fingers are stiff now, and delight in the lovely autumn blaze that would envelop her friend. If she were pregnant, which seems to be the case, the wedding would be even more agreeable. Gabrielle, who had just obtained her master's degree and was about to become a research assistant in the Université de Montréal sociology department, in other words a marker of student papers, would make allowances for tradition, last refuge of the higher classes. And the fact remained that she believed she truly liked Guylaine, plump and brunette, who had not been born to white niggers of America, but was that her fault?

Bone cancer carried Guylaine away in a matter of weeks nine years later. Another wolf perhaps, the beast that had eaten away at her soul since the birth of the twins, a boy and a girl without grace, dull-witted since their first cry. Guylaine removed herself from the road where they were growing up the wrong way, she refused all chemicals, and Gabrielle blames herself for having been kind enough to understand her, and thus to have tolerated her apathy. "But bone cancer is always fast," she tells herself, to shake off the shadow that could let remorse seep in.

She samples from the basket the season's last strawberries, the hulls come away between her teeth, warm, smearing lips and fingers, one of those sensual pleasures that should have been enough to keep Guylaine attached to life.

She didn't die in strawberry season. She died one October afternoon at the Hotel-Dieu, skeletal and absent, hydrated through her veins, under the scarcely bereft eyes of her children, her parents, Fernand and Gabrielle, who had torn herself away from the orientation meeting of the party in which the young sociologist was establishing a reputation for being a most useful analyst. It hadn't taken much to make her nearly pretty — contact lenses, a light permanent to give some life to her ultrafine hair, the pleasure of having published a few articles in one of the papers, a few emotionally painful lovers, though there'd been none that autumn. The death was serene. Nearly nothing — a gasp, then hands squeezed, vague gratitude to the doctor who'd had to step up the dose of morphine. They all had cars, they would meet at the funeral when the date and time had been set.

A week before, Gabrielle had had half an hour alone with Guylaine early one night. The dying were allowed unlimited visitors, and that time was as good as any other for a friend whose days were so full, in fact she was sure she was helping to relieve the anguish which must be terrible in the hospital dark. She helped Guylaine to drink through a straw, in a covered glass like the ones now sold for babies. She'd had to bring her ear close to her friend's white lips to take in, through her disgusting breath, her whisper. Stanzas as slow as a heat wave, piercing as a blizzard. "I detest you. You ruined my youth. You ignored my children. You sneered at my husband. You seduced my father."

He had revealed it to her, weeping, in the early days of this cancer, begging her to forgive him for having caressed her friend who had undressed in front of him years ago, while he was reading Bernanos and paying no attention to the languorous melody she was tinkling on the piano. If Gabrielle had said nothing, betrayed nothing, it was, so he said, because she had wanted it all, beneath her intellectual manner she was a whore, she was always exposing a thigh, a breast, when she came to the house. One day, he could swear, she wasn't wearing panties under her miniskirt, he was the only one to have noticed, if he had mentioned it to his daughter and his wife they'd have thought he was crazy. He had in fact remained crazy about Gabrielle whom he'd dreamed so much of entering. If only she had given him the chance, this story would have ended, he'd have been a father to his daughter, a grandfather to his grandchildren, a husband to his wife. Perhaps Guylaine's bones would have stayed healthy, it wasn't normal, this punishment imprinted on a young woman. His daughter. It was his own diverted sperm that was muddled up.

He was ugly and trembling, he had asked her for secrecy because it was too late and he didn't want any drama during his child's last days. But she, the dying woman, knew very well that he was still trying to keep up the old desire that continued to swell, that she was dealing with two obscenities, one of whom wouldn't come to see her five times before the end. And then, because she was Guylaine, she had given in, again. She would talk when no one could hear her, when Gabrielle could simply shrug and close a white door on a shadow that peed in its adult diaper, under a sheet as dry as her bones.

She had one final hiss, at the moment when she knew that Gabrielle had had enough. "There's one thing you won't have. The one you want."

What do I want? Gabrielle wondered, as she finished off the memory of the pharmacist who may have been right to think she was offering herself. She hadn't worn a bra that day, it had been pleasant to feel her nipples becoming erect and her belly pressing against that hard thing which she didn't yet know how to name, and to grow old exciting him from afar, though she doesn't remember going to his place without panties, except during the period of long Moroccan robes, and he wouldn't have been able to see anything.

What was it I wanted? she thinks that evening, crammed with the play of a man who is still adolescent. Before her, the Rivière des Prairies, which are no longer prairies but fields of bungalows and towers that are also crammed with seniors in small apartments, the pink streak of the sun dying drowsily over Montreal, the horizon barred all the way to the United States. The strata of a country about which some wrote poems at the time when she did or did not wear panties under a miniskirt or a long robe that had come from Africa, like the words of Frantz Fanon.

THREE

AN ORDINARY HANDSAW could have cut up what remained of the two caraganas planted at the beginning of June and dead in August. But the contractor arrived with a small excavator, chainsaws and two workers, through some misunderstanding that's still unsolved, if Gabrielle is to judge by the chorus of curses rising from the lawn.

With the powerful voice of a skinny man, the owner of the garden-level apartment declares that they must also remove the hedge of honeysuckle, it grows like a weed and blocks the view of the river, its roots are so tenacious that drastic measures are called for. The owners' meeting, he claims, had agreed on the principle of putting in low plants so that people on the garden level (even though, as he doesn't add, they've paid less for their three rooms and kitchen) can enjoy the building's interesting location as much as the people on the upper floors. As proof, he brings up the caraganas with their twisted trunks, whose thin, drooping branches should have grown low and broad if the acid soil hadn't killed them so quickly.

From the fourth floor Gabrielle hears only the rumbling of the debate — including the indignant barbs of Fatima, who hasn't been ordered to make the honeysuckle disappear and who dares to confront the mule-headed man. Pierre is familiar with the quarrel because he's heard it more clearly from his place. He tells Gabrielle when he arrives that she should watch out for that Monsieur Poupart. "His wife has one cheek purple from a burn, she'd spilled a bottle of oil and to punish her he set fire to it and she won't lodge a complaint." In his opinion, it's the husband who killed the caraganas by pretending to water them during the summer drought, who knows what mixture he was using? Honeysuckle can take anything, it's common.

Long after the workers have gone, leaving the hedge intact, angry hissing rises up from the terrace of apartment 101, where the brute tells his wife at length about what he plans to do. Like a saw, he in turn disturbs the morning air, which had been washed by a cooler night, at last.

In the yard, the cutting has been done cleanly, the remains of the trunks blend with the mulch, the tired grass appears to have been tonsured for some autumnal ceremony, Gabrielle tells Pierre, who doesn't understand the image. "What's a tonsure?" She laughs at this child who has never known priests. He's better off that way. Besides, the last one she'd known had brought bad luck.

"It's a sign of chastity," she said. Though she knows nothing about it. She assumes that the ridiculous shaving of the top of the head was intended to lessen desire for women. Surely it's hard to caress a man whose brain has been denuded by some old bishop dressed like a vestal virgin. His kisses must reek of the void.

Pierre inquires about that last priest she'd known.

She wouldn't swear that Damien Perreault had been an abbé, despite the premature baldness that suggested it, as well as what he gave her to understand about a stay at the monastery of Saint-Gildas-de-Rhuys, in Brittany, where he had apparently been introduced to the teachings of the monk Abélard. Saint-Gildas was a small seaside resort with a handful of inns that were more inviting than its austere abbey, and Gabrielle had trouble picturing Damien as a reader in the refectory. Rather, she saw him devouring a book on medieval philosophy at the beach, coated with luxurious suntan oil, between two naps in the sun. He did seem to know all there was to know about Abélard, having thoroughly penetrated that vanity so brilliant it had become theological, that faith in oneself that really does turn certain men into images of the God they've created to invite comparison. That would have been Damien's style, had he persevered. But he also talked about cliffs, sea spray, jellyfish with as much precision as the teachings of Abélard, with whom the encounter finally seemed more like a vacation affair than a mystical experience before an altar. Moreover he'd said nothing about Héloïse, whose spirit seemed to Gabrielle, from the little she'd read about her, more riveting than that of her illustrious seducer.

"Damien always lied," she says. And at that moment she senses, as if it were in her windpipe, the slight bitterness he exuded when he was talking to her, that flowed only in her, it had taken her months to understand why.

She sends Pierre back to his work, the rest he wouldn't understand at all.

Damien and Gabrielle had been colleagues at the university, vague adversaries at the beginning of the school year, having quarrelled over the only course on class structure offered in Quebec. The period of strikes was over, but there was still plenty of fraternization between the few supervised hours of teaching. It had all started in the office of the dean, who was very tall, very handsome, very silent. They were drinking manhattans. Present were Damien, pink-faced after one sip, skinny Alexandre, whose wife would wait for him, and Serge, trying to discipline them into a six p.m. meeting with plans for another the next morning. Gabrielle had worn a blue wool dress, the blue of the dean's eyes, with a full-length zipper nearly to her boots, which girls wore all day and from which they never managed to scrape off all the salt from the streets. Alexandre was talking about women's underwear as a gauge of the changing times, he claimed he often cheated on his wife. Gabrielle played scatterbrained because of that blue which was suddenly unbearable, ice turned to silk to be torn between her and the tall silent boy. Never would she be virginal enough for him. Something evil was alighting, radiant, at the end of her twentieth year.

Damien had seized the moment before they did, he had filled the glasses, spattered some paper by suddenly raising his, challenged Gabrielle to take off her clothes to test Alexandre's thesis. With a sharp tug of her zipper she'd done so. A few seconds and a few centimetres of the bra-slip she was so fond of, that pushed up her small breasts in a double layer of lace which she washed by hand with expensive soap flakes in the hope of preserving it for a long time. It was only when half-naked that she was somewhat beautiful. And now there was at least that between them, this perfect waste.

The blue did not break, it even became the first laugh in the love of a lifetime, one she would never recount.

But Damien wouldn't rest during the months and years when he would be their mutual friend, until he tried to have a go at this miracle, marvelling at having been the first witness while pretending to be its guardian.

He was also a visitor to the home of the married lover, reporting to Gabrielle the colours of the house and of the children's curls, their mealtimes, all those bits of answers to the questions that she didn't ask. Little by little, in front of the Alexandres and Serges, he had even played at being Gabrielle's lover, they all got drawn into that *trompe l'oeil*, as a favour to the lovers. One night, at the faculty Christmas party, Damien had groped her in front of her colleagues until she'd thought that he really was interested and tried to console him afterwards, in the car where they were sobering up while they waited for some heat. He had kissed the tips

of her fingers as one might do to some inconsequential trol-
lop. From his blank expression during the drive home, she
realized that she was just the proxy for his own love of the
same boy.

That was the only chilly episode between them. Afterwards, she let him kiss the other man's juices on her neck,
seek in her the trace of stolen bliss and breathe in the unhappiness of absence. The hours, at least, were filled.

It was Damien who had signed her up for the sovereigntist party he'd been associated with since its beginning. The
adopted son of quiet bourgeois, he was, he said, the natural
son of a former Nazi who'd found refuge in Canada, who
had tracked down his son who was also the son of a whore
and left him a fortune of dubious origin, which Damien
chose to spend discreetly and had put at the service of the
democrats in our liberation movement, after associating for
a while with terrorists, the first ones to have finally drawn
some lessons from our history. Those who favoured violence
were all poor and neurotic, he said, and you had to be
healthy and rich to have a normal relationship with freedom. And so he'd left them, after his sojourn for reflection at
Saint-Gildas, and he had given some energy in the form of
cash to the petits bourgeois hungry for a normal state, the
kind that are respected by the newsmagazines and are
the only ones that matter.

Why had she believed that nonsense? Because he spouted
it without the usual hesitation of our local thinkers? Because
he read *Der Spiegel* in the original and summarized brilliantly all the French and American periodicals piled up on
the backseat of his comfortable Citroën? In any case, she had
developed a liking for the topicality of things. And had got
it into her head that palingenesis couldn't come about without the commitment of people like her, who understood the

source and the term. Or so we believe at the dawn of our thirties, in a country where bombs no longer go off and where intellectuals socially on the rise nonetheless owe something to the neurotics who are in jail. She had acquired a membership card, paid more than her dues, and started to attend meetings.

Damien wanted to stay in the shadows but to make Gabrielle, who had a way with people, into a figure. That was how he put it. While she was spending her evenings on a detailed dissection, in the original, of Rosa Luxemburg's relationship with nationalism, persuading herself against all evidence that it hadn't been a total repudiation, Damien extricated from hundreds of newspapers and magazines signs of a rebirth of patriotism, and it was from them that she finally drew her arguments, around party tables where there was no time to waste on debates about the particular circumstances of the Spartacus League in the early years of the century.

Little by little, Gabrielle had shed the jargon of her discipline, preserving only her admiration for that little bit of a woman whose speeches had galvanized men and who hadn't feared the police. One day she would go to Berlin and sit on the edge of the canal where murderers had thrown Rosa's corpse.

Gabrielle's students now found her more fiery, they were glad to see dispelled the dissertationlike atmosphere that she'd previously felt required to keep up. The same was true in the party, where some were beginning to think she had the makings of a *pasionaria*. Not the kind of which leaders are made, a woman was out of the question, but the kind that strikes the proper vein among party members.

There was a small triumph one Sunday morning at a National Council meeting, one that would bolster the development of her political career. A confrontation with the

Maoists had been brewing for weeks, there were still a few — people of speeches and spirit who wanted to make the party into a ferment of proletarian revolution in North America, a place where the future would be not only French, but fair. She led a workshop organized with the help of Damien's notes. "You think," she told them in some introductory remarks, "that there's a country dedicated to revenge and justice, a country that will not lay down its arms, that will not lay down its spirit until there is a global confrontation. You think that three hundred years of European energy are being wiped out, that the Chinese era is beginning. Mao reminds you of the power of emperors, but he is actually a carapace covered with rust, like those army leaders you see at funeral processions or abandoned in the sorghum fields where the Chinese people toil. Mao is nothing but a solitary shadow, watching and hoping for the twilight of a world. Proletariats will join capitalist states as has happened in Russia and the United States. Mao is old, he's watching the revolution slip away while he shields his eyes from the sun. With him, you would take a great leap into the void."

It was clear to see that she read, that such literary considerations weren't spontaneous. But in a party that cared about an image of culture she really did stand out as someone who knew how to write, who could carry on a conversation with the few political tourists from France who were coming more and more often to look into the effervescence of their picturesque American cousins. Without altogether retreating, the Maoists had changed halls. The Great Helmsman would die a few months later, in a climate of revolutionary rust that she certainly hadn't been alone in pointing out, but the party recognized her instinct as being reliable enough that she was entrusted with other missions on the ideas front.

On the day after Mao's funeral, the university's internal mail brought her an anonymous missive: "Young Woman, I too have read page 561 in André Malraux's *Antimémoires*, Folio paperback number 23, Gallimard, 1972. Fear not, I wish only good things for you and for Quebec's independence, I shall respect the secret of your brilliant inspiration."

Gabrielle had not read Malraux. She immediately obtained a copy and on page 561 found, nearly word for word, the text that Damien had written for her. There was fog between the lines, and lessons that would serve her well, later on, in the company of other liars. She didn't waste time hating Damien before she confronted him in his sun-bathed office where he was reading an article on Kissinger's strategy in *Foreign Policy*. Barely did his plump priestly cheeks turn pink, as they did during their alcohol-fuelled chatter. He took so many notes on so many subjects, he said, that he could easily have copied out passages from *Antimémoires* two or three years ago and inadvertently incorporated them into something he'd written himself. She could use the same excuse if anyone complained, it happened to so many professors, apparently Malraux himself liked nothing better than to heighten facts by seasoning them with lies. She shouldn't be so puritanical, as people learned in abbeys.

What did he know about Malraux? He didn't read many books. She realized that when he copied, it was cheating. From that day on she separated what she wrote from what Damien did and put herself in a condition of infidelity.

She now saw him only in the elegant restaurants to which he was fond of inviting her, where he behaved like a regular, where he drank too much of wines that were too fine. She went along as if she were going to a show, for the wild stories about his life to which he managed to give some verisimilitude.

Over noisettes of venison at Postel, he had claimed to be the owner of hunting grounds in the Camargue to which he went incognito, because local descendants of the partisans would slit the throat of this son of a Nazi who had taken advantage of a miserly old woman to appropriate the property legally.

Over champagne in an elegant Vermont inn, where it had pleased him to drive her some hundred and fifty kilometres in the snow, he had given himself a brother in the States, a rather famous ophthalmologist, whose wife had become Damien's lover in room thirteen of this charming retreat; of it had been born a daughter as beautiful as the daylight but deaf and blind, the mother had been shattered by grief, she would die soon.

Over tea in the Ritz garden he had told her he'd recently become engaged to a Toronto actress, daughter of a ruined Greek ship owner who had made a new fortune in Canada by selling copies of Hellenic sculptures to the nouveaux riches with swimming pools, with whom the Queen City abounded.

He was always coming back from amazing trips, from hotels that no guidebook had spotted, routes that no one else had followed, encounters that no one else could imagine and that gave him information on how foreigners viewed Quebec sovereignty — with hostility, in general. The worst was yet to come, he repeated again and again, Gabrielle should be on her guard.

She listened as if she believed him, she knew how to make those eyes. Just as she knew that Damien was as afraid of planes as of women, which demolished all his lies at the outset. But he was a contrast with the pale creatures she met in the department, shadows of their borrowed ideas, brains hesitant under the greasy hair that soiled the pillows of their unsatisfied girlfriends. He carried her along too, most often away from the party militants who adopted the missionary position both in bed and in their political sermons, unversed in either the subtleties of the flesh or the perversions of the powerful. The shadows Damien talked about were false, but they were more real than the hopes that rang out in the fleur-de-lys flags those political enthusiasts waved.

One late-summer evening, at one of the new terraces on Saint-Denis Street whose vulgarity Damien deplored, Gabrielle told him that she'd requested an unpaid leave from the university and that she was going to run in a north-end Montreal riding. She had spent her childhood there, still had some useful ties, liked places on the river. The party thought it had a chance there, though they were all aware of the limits to popular support for the idea of sovereignty. She herself wasn't even sure that she altogether believed in it, she told Damien, but increasingly she preferred meeting with adults more than with students barely out of adolescence. Their hopeless ignorance had come after their insolent ignorance, she was a good enough pedagogue but preferred to exercise her talents on people less impudent and more cheerful, who would address her respectfully. What's more, like everyone else, Quebec's sheep-like history turned her stomach. In the universities, it was forgotten. But on the streets of her childhood, how many people still thought that the genuine God, if he spoke to humans, would have done so in English, and that it was incumbent on them to put up with it?

Damien's expression became intractable before she had finished her third sentence. "You're crazy. Not only will you lose the election — as will the party — you'll wreck your own life too. Rumours will spread about your married lover — or lovers. You won't be able to withstand them. You don't have the nerves for debate. You can't write a good speech that's clear and succinct. Besides, I know the party activists, they won't even support your nomination." There was a threat in his voice. On his chubby face small wrinkles were appearing, signs of near old age, unattractive. In a moment, she had grasped everything. That he thought he could hold on to her. That she was merely a cog in the machinery for transmitting his stories to the other man, to the person he wanted to continue interesting through her. That he could see her getting away, leaving the triangle, occupying the stage by herself. She realized that he was the author of the anonymous letter, that he'd wanted to be the bird of ill omen at the beginning of her public life, while playing the role of her lover. One day, at a moment of victory, he would tell all, he would betray her.

And so, with no outside teaching, she absorbed the first rule of her new life: to get the perverts on her side. Instead of appearing wounded, she asked him for advice. At the second cognac, he thought he still had her. His colour came back. And until he became the wreck whose colleagues took over his courses when he was in detox, she treated him as a scout.

Which happened every now and then, when he was in the capital. He came for her in luxurious limousines of a kind the government no longer allowed cabinet ministers, they would go to Serge Bruyère, where nouvelle cuisine offered *civet de lapin* with a blueberry coulis, they would wash down Damien's latest fantasies with the finest Pouilly, they'd be seated near tables of Americans, to shield their conversations.

One night of black ice on the maze of highways that run out of the overly old city, he told her that he was going to New York for treatment of a mysterious sickness in his blood. She could only see the red blotches settling into a face that was barely puffy, she pretended to believe him, as usual. He disappeared for six months though and only resurfaced for a brief call to her place at dawn. He was after a job in a French university, he was going to set himself up overseas to reconnect with his origins, a letter of recommendation from a minister of cultural affairs would enhance his file, everyone knows how sensitive the French are to the proper connections. Gabrielle was annoyed. She had learned to be sparing with her signature for fear of abuse by sycophants and most of all, she didn't want circulating in France, one of the rare countries to befriend her government, proof of her relationship with an individual as disturbed as Damien. And what if there were some basis to his story about a Nazi father? She gained some time by asking for a copy of his c.v. so she could put useful comments into her recommendation. He hung up with promises to send it. She knew that such a document had never existed, Damien's curriculum vitae existed only in the current of his dreams.

The following week, on a day of thaw and mud all the way to the Parliament, she learned through Marguerite, a mutual friend, that Damien had been found in front of the fireplace in a chalet he'd rented in Sainte-Adèle. He hadn't paid the rent since December, he was in debt beyond all measure, he had defied his cirrhosis to the point of confusing codeine and cognac, sleep and death. It would be called suicide.

He had left nothing for Gabrielle, neither a message nor anything in his will, because there wasn't one, the copy of Malraux's *Antimémoires* having like everything else taken the road to a secondhand book store. Any sign would have been a gesture of the kind that are invented for novels. But Damien couldn't have done that, he'd been exhausted.

At the burial — they were maybe a dozen at the Cimetière

de l'Est, near the oil refineries, in the shadow of depressing apartment buildings — she saw an old woman who was crying and who looked like Damien. His mother, the only one. She saw a young woman who was crying and who looked like a photo. The Toronto actress, or the American girl, or a new secretary in the sociology department to whom he had often given flowers. Just one friend, anyway, which Gabrielle no longer was. She had made him incidental to her love and to her work. In the end, she had been more skilled at betrayal than he was.

These were things that she thought about for the first time in the shadow of the so strange presence of Pierre. She touched the railing from which the warmth of the day was withdrawing but which still held the memory of the sun. Since that time the only place in Quebec that upset her was the square of crabgrass where Damien was rotting, where there wasn't even a tombstone. She'd gone back there often.

FOUR

IN MOST MONTREAL neighbourhoods they still ring the angelus even though no one hears it. The angel of the Lord does not however descend onto rue des Bouleaux, in Laval, because the apartment buildings there were built on meadows where only yesterday the clinking of cowbells could be heard, far from the villages and their churches. It wouldn't have occurred to anyone to put up a house of worship in the vicinity, not even the sects that are beginning to prosper further north, in the folds of the Laurentians. Here, everything is neat and tidy, even inside the residents' heads; for a long time they've been spending Sundays cooking or cleaning, they hope for an easing of Sunday store hours so they can do their shopping before taking in a movie at the mall, it would be more convenient.

Gabrielle knows that it's noon though when the door of a pearl grey Cadillac that belongs to the sister of a lady on the third floor slams in the visitors' parking lot. Whenever it's sunny the two women lunch together on the balcony. Gabrielle's view of them is from above and too close. They are tanned like the Floridians they become in winter, with backcombed hair of greenish blond, heavy shoulders bare under tank tops meant for teenagers, bodies preserved in a certain age. Look-alikes, maybe twins, though their voices clash. The visitor speaks coarsely, the other woman softly, so what makes its way up to Gabrielle is an odd monologue, one-half of a conversation, like telephone scenes on TV soaps. Most of the time in fact they seem to be chatting about programs they watched the day before, their delivery is not disturbing, it's the smooth rhythm of a spool, barely broken by the clinking of cutlery.

What's most remarkable to Gabrielle is the roundness of the scene. They have never cast a curious glance at her own balcony, at the little scandal, within reach of their understanding, that is the presence of Pierre. He doesn't touch her except in late afternoon, moments of tender and silent fornication that already are starting to feel like the rendezvous of old lovers. But still, he seems settled in and a little too bare, decent ladies could whisper when they see him. But they are absorbed in one another, exchange polite small talk, serve one another juice and water, salads and cakes that are always topped with mounds of ice cream. They don't laugh, they chat on and on, they're fond of each other. Around two p.m. the car door slams again, the neighbour doesn't reappear on the balcony, maybe she uses the afternoon to put together food for the morrow, no detail is superfluous for one who cares about harmony.

"I knew a senator," says Gabrielle, "who had the very same car." It was the last of the Cadillacs with any style or presence, the rear end bulging like the cushion of a marchioness, the leather buffed to stir a woman's sex, the dashboard cut from mahogany like an ocean liner's, the nose of the hood like a diadem, contemptuous of the ordinary people on the road, those with small engines. The senator of course was tiny, he seemed just rich enough to be appalled by all the rumours and to pray that God would preserve him from louts. One of whom Gabrielle would have been had she not been a woman before being a separatist, a race that he thought he abhorred.

She had met him and seduced him, but chastely, during the first televised debate of the election campaign. Her victory was a foregone conclusion; she was slender and fresh, filled with the grace of the words of the future, *dignity* being the most powerful, a subtle reminder of the humiliations that were still too frequent and of the immense pleasure to be gained from making Canada stick to its false promises when the time came. Time wasn't urgent, she said in a voice of velvet, we'll take what we need to bow out graciously, and while we wait we will better confirm our modernity. Was she not the very image of youth and of the skills henceforth asserting themselves in French to the four corners of the territory?

The host from the public network favoured her side and the little man, who had become a senator through business, not politics, who was discovering the new situation of women under the spotlights, stammered banalities about the good will of Canadians. Still, he lost the match with elegance and invited her to lunch at the Mas des Oliviers. Out of the dimness, where jurists of all tendencies still drank martinis before their *bavette à l'échalote*, rose a distinct sound, the sound of the west end of the city, of money duly counted. Men entered in twos and threes, coatless despite the September chill, they would nod in the direction of a table, stop at another, murmur greetings laden with complicity. One could gauge their status from the time it took them to get to their seats and on how long the route was, a geography far more complex than what's discussed in sociology texts where status is however a seminal notion, one that is measured with the greatest obsessiveness and with instruments that are constantly being refined. There were lawyers who advised investors, lawyers who created numbered companies into which they poured investors' money, lawyers who served as intermediaries between investors, lawyers who merged investors' assets and lawyers who'd become investors themselves, by dint of having been there when the bill appeared, the high point of their day. Across from Gabrielle was a man who had used the various categories of lawyers and who was therefore greeted by nearly all of them, except for those newly minted who would have appreciated an introduction. Among these young people a few women formed as did she a bright, nearly damp spot, one of those moist breezes that on the shores of the St. Lawrence announce so certainly the end of summer.

No one in these circles knew her, the program wouldn't be aired until the following day. They must have thought that the senator, long unattached, was trying to get back in shape. It was the impression he gave in fact, he was attentive, gallant, already tamed. Gabrielle drank white wine, which placed her on the borderline between virginal and brazen, and she was enjoying a *filet de doré meunière*, a fish that does not fear butter, thus allying sobriety and seduction. She was clearly displaying a sound instinct, including that for pleasing her contradictor by asking him to tell her about the people and the place. He was not as banal as he'd been in the studio, he even sparkled behind his round glasses. To hear him talk, the diners were nearly all cuckolds, and the most fortunate in business were the two tall grey-haired ones at the back, whose recent merger was so perfect that their wives were already sleeping together and were even sharing a well-known actress. Gabrielle discovered that, as well as being a direct route for advancing one's ideas, politics was the most fascinating of kaleidoscopes.

The senator became one of her amused companions in the other camp, of whom she learned to have many, with no ulterior motive, for the fun of it. It was harmless to spend time with them, to laugh with them, to get in their cars along the Ottawa–Montreal–Quebec City corridor and to inquire about their families or their love lives. After all, the future of Quebec was not a matter of life and death. No one was the enemy and one had to wish for others what they were reluctant to wish for themselves, what they'd be happy to have when the time came. They were getting old, she thought, and they were afraid of the wind. She had the energy to cleave it for them.

Heady weeks that brought her party to victory, contrary to all expectations, by accident. Not once while she crisscrossed her future riding, overcoming her jitters before making some speech or other at some meeting or other, even a friendly one, was she really prepared for the wild notion of winning a seat in the National Assembly and for a government that would be hers. For the thought of handing over her course outlines to a replacement, along with the keys to her office, of renting a furnished apartment on rue Sainte-Ursule, of memorizing train and plane schedules along with the names of her new colleagues, all of them as stunned as she was on the night of the victory. The bottom of her heart, that blue place where she formed an island with her lover, felt solemn and emotional. They only needed to work well and the country would be within reach.

She knew Quebec City from reading Adrienne Choquette's novel *Laure Clouet* and she remembered the first chapter as clearly as if she herself had been the woman whose youth was in suspense, who on an early September day like this, from a stone house with a fenced-in garden across from the provincial museum "went out, wearing kidskin gloves and a gabardine suit." It was dove-coloured alpaca, the suit that she wore for the swearing-in, the skirt too tame, her hair too well-coiffed, she was surprised to hear herself say aloud, "So help me God," when she intended to erase the last sign of God, preventer of all women, from cultural affairs, the ministry entrusted to her.

The ministry building, tall and grey on the Grande Allée,

overlooked what had been the world of Laure Clouet, and during the few weeks when she was still anonymous, Gabrielle liked to walk there, filled with the old silence that seeped from the homes. Deserted by the good burghers and transformed into restaurants with atmosphere, in the morning they possessed the haughty blindness that made Quebec the most Pharisaic of cities with class, slower than any other in America to uncorset its daughters and to demand fewer lies of its sons. Gabrielle, who was preparing to bring together the best minds of the province to write the most audacious and the most complete proposals for cultural policy, inhaled the last residues of the constraints that she would disperse, smiled at still-unknown bureaucrats, had few doubts and, unlike Laure Clouet, didn't wear gloves.

At least not until the December winds, they were vicious and laden with all the revenge of the ancestors. The mood turned grey then, even in the trains that week after week took her back to Montreal. The Saturday arts sections, while more tolerant of her than of her predecessors, were already finding plenty to fault in her policy outlines, mocking their ambitiousness for such a small people. The writers thought their chatter was harmless enough, but it weighed heavily in the government's faint understanding of anything cultural.

It took less than six months for the area in front of 225 de la Grande Allée Est and the side entrance to the Parliament to erase Quebec City's charm. She no longer saw the beauty of the stones, she travelled past the fortifications in a limousine, liked only the bridges across the St. Lawrence. She enjoyed some success, particularly at the beginning. She had an instinct for maintaining equidistance between heritage preservation and support for the avant-garde, though she had little time to read, or to understand where she was heading.

On the eve of a federal-provincial conference she was happy to meet up with the senator in Ottawa. In his discreet *pied-à-terre* on the tenth floor of a tower on Metcalfe Street, he was as anonymous as the Quebec minister of cultural affairs, who was surprised to find agreeable and teasing the notion of a transgression on federalist turf. Time would weigh less heavily up there. Champagne, smoked salmon, Russian bread, even caviar obtained from who knows what embassy: he had prepared well for the pause.

His name was Champfleur, a ridiculous one for a man reputed to be grim, though he did have a silky way of shaking hands. He settled her — deliberately, it seemed to her — in the *voltaire* chair with too many studs that sat next to his enormous library, the kind that seems to have been purchased by the metre by parvenus. But she was wrong to think that. While he was attending to his platters, she saw that what he had assembled there was a sizeable collection of the world's poetry, meticulously bound, ordered, filed in our two original or translated languages. Nothing else.

She asked the most idiotic of questions.

"Have you read them all?"

There was irritation in his smile. "I tell ladies, or young ladies, that I have no more need to read all these books than they need to wear all their jewels."

But he soon took pity. "Anyway, I see that you wear very few." It would have taken more kindly remarks to mitigate Gabrielle's feelings of inadequacy, she who had come to cultural affairs without knowing personally a single poet, much less an entire opus, except for bits that had been made into songs. As for the troubadours of the land who celebrated its powerful panoramas and assigned its animal might to its men, she kept them to one side. Sociology makes one invulnerable to collective illusions, to anthropomorphic drift, even if it's carried along by the most beautiful music. If she believed in the rebirth of Quebec it was through other forms of progress than those that accompany grand sentiments.

While he was pouring inexhaustible champagne and teaching her how cream and black bread together had been setting off sturgeon eggs since the time when French singers were at once rending and refining Russian hearts, Étienne Champfleur talked to her about the importance of poetry, of which he read very little.

"My walls are cushioned with words. I have close at hand when I need it all the ways, brilliant or naive, to express all the states of mind and body of a lifetime, and several lifetimes wouldn't be enough. They are there, I'm sure of it, they have existed and sometimes still exist, in other places. I like owning them, the way others amass great wines that they don't drink. Besides, we couldn't taste them. We have had the misfortune, you and I, to be born into a world immunized against tragedy. Here, all of us can consummate our loves before we lose them, which makes the loss less painful, and we die from accident or disease, at a normal age most of the time. Horrors are rare, we experience them by proxy. I will even tell you that you're right to steer clear of our poets, their greatest tragedy is not to have one, and to use words like forceps to bring them into being. They lack agitation, cruelty, they have nothing to do with them. I've classified them separately, with their calculated sadness. I'll change my mind, I'll follow you when just one of them is overjoyed with our mediocrity, with being the Job of our own dung heap."

He fell silent. She didn't really understand. The champagne blunted her attention, and while she thought she'd understood a warning against strong emotions, she was suddenly very unhappy, or allowed herself to become so at this time of night, so far from everything she thought she hoped for. She was not yet forty years old, her body was a minor parenthesis in her lover's life, poetry was a wall in a strange house, in a stubborn city. Power was beginning to please her and she knew that that was bad. Tomorrow, others would compose for her statements as hollow as those of her adolescence, and she would enjoy the press conference game. How could she hate herself more than that? By knowing, like our poets, that you don't kill yourself over such a thing. That there would never be enough pain in the entire lifetime of a bus driver's daughter, now a cabinet minister, for her to die of it.

She drank far too much and cried just as much, in the dim light of a little man who didn't even hold her hand. He was content to become the bespectacled senator again, who, to help Gabrielle regain her composure around midnight, the hour when she should go back to the Château Laurier if she wanted to arrive at the conference centre a little fresh, inquired about her new life in the other capital, amused at the similarities between the vanities of the two parliaments, told her that a few days earlier he'd overheard a conversation over Sauternes and foie gras at Café Burger in Hull, between the Montreal president of a major bank and the federal finance minister; they'd been assessing the effect on separatist feelings of a threat to move the head office of the institution that had been established in Quebec at the turn of the twentieth century. "Their minds may be twisted," the senator agreed, "but they have a better hand than you do." While she waited for an Ottawa taxi, a rarity at night in this well-behaved little town, Gabrielle caught herself debating with some brio.

The federal–provincial conference had as usual left no perceptible public trace except some awkwardness between

Gabrielle Perron and Étienne Champfleur. They saw one another now and then, on the neutral ground of restaurants, and they stuck to parliamentary gossip. The senator was useful to Gabrielle all the same, with what he gleaned from remarks in the federal capital, which had been throbbing with nerves since the separatists had come to power. Some said they were in the service of a foreign power, it was known through the Canadian mistresses of French diplomats, others claimed to be taking part in highly intelligent meetings to prepare for infiltrating enemy ranks in the very heart of the Quebec capital. Rue d'Auteuil would soon be bristling with microphones, the senator said, amused. She repeated little of this nonsense to her colleagues, who wouldn't have appreciated her relationship with a man who belonged to money and Canada.

Their last meeting took place in Quebec City in the fall, at the Closerie des Lilas, which was to the Upper Town what the Mas des Oliviers was to the centre of Montreal, with the addition of some senior government officials. Thin, emaciated almost, Champfleur alluded to the doctor he'd come to consult, one of the leading Canadian specialists in prostate disorders. It was no longer fitting to smile at it, to imagine that in another life, before the Cadillac, the little man could have been a charming, lanky lover, one of those who can hold back their pleasure for hours, probe a girl so thoroughly and gently that she is only a sex, afterwards taking his in her mouth, grateful. He was the father of three sons, all in business and scattered to other provinces, he rarely had anything to say about them, or about their mother who early on had flown off to New York with someone richer and less intelligent than he was.

At the Closerie he drank only water, and that had limited confidences. She asked Jean-Charles to drive him to the airport, she was in a hurry, she'd go back to the ministry by taxi, to prepare for the public hearings that had finally been called to study her cultural policy. The worst of the winds made her take her leave very quickly, she had on thin shoes and the sidewalk was icy.

Two months later she heard of his death on the radio and though she was in Montreal on the day of the funeral, she didn't put in an appearance at the Saint-Jean-Baptiste church, the false cathedral of Plateau-Mont-Royal, where he had been born, son of a storekeeper. From the death notice in *Le Devoir* she learned that he'd also had a daughter, Gabrielle, a teacher and poet, dead at thirty. But she hadn't had time to go and greet an entourage now indifferent, the man had been such a loner. The party caucus was shut away for two days in a downtown hotel, a kind of meditation before the upcoming battle of the referendum on sovereignty; it was unthinkable for the minister of cultural affairs, who was being counted on to rally the artistic community and to find words for the most memorable slogans, to turn up, out of place, at a gathering, even an obscure one, of opponents.

She didn't even know in which cemetery he had been buried. She thought that now she had plenty of time to make inquires, to place a rose on his grave or even, if it wasn't too late in the summer, to plant a perennial. After all, the match between them was a tie — nothing they had debated had reached a conclusion, twisted minds on all sides had manipulated the fearful, who held the fate of the world in their dried-up brains and constantly postponed deciding what it was until the morrow. It was indeed impossible for the poets to extricate any images from this limbo, the only truly lasting inheritance of the catechism. They were no more inspiring than the junkyards that the country was full of, which were beginning to be recycled into flea markets.

What had become of his library? He'd had the intelligence, or the pity, to bequeath it to someone other than Gabrielle, or to the National Library of Canada, which prided itself on assembling a world-class compilation but whose poetry collection, save for the required legal deposit in our two languages, was until then very limited. Few would note it because few had complained.

FIVE

A FIRE IS AN EVENT far less spectacular today than it was during Gabrielle's childhood, when there were regular conflagrations, winter and summer, with the tremendous noise of blazes swallowing up the possessions of large families and sometimes one of the children, who would be found under his little iron bed, burned to death. The entire school would then file past the gilt-handled ivory coffin that would take the dead child to paradise. Long after the firemen had left, the bowels of the kitchen could still be made out, with walls where hung, miraculously, a holy picture or a calendar. And over the following days, the victims had time to force their way cautiously to the cellar, where they would recover the useless objects relegated there. If it was January, the month most conducive to overheating, the place would be devastated until spring, and the dead child's soul would remain frozen in the vicinity — an object lesson for young smokers of the cigarettes to which many of these disasters were attributed, to the unrelenting shame of their parents who often had to resign themselves to fleeing to other neighbourhoods.

There was nothing like that in the new suburbs. If the fire had been caused by smoking, as might have been the case in a neighbouring house that night, it was easily contained thanks to the fire-retardant materials used nowadays for sofas and mattresses; it was very rare now for a bed to become a child's tomb. And in the event of more serious negligence — cooking fat catching fire or the improper use of some electrical appliance — the flames rarely went beyond the inside walls, stopped by the increasingly effective firewalls required by law. Television still showed the occasional sequence of a carnage that had decimated a family, but they nearly always took place in the country, to people who were not only impoverished and poorly housed, but also careless. In Laval, in a neighbourhood such as rue des Bouleaux, people had at most been wakened by sirens around three a.m. Only two homes had been briefly evacuated and in less than a week the traces of soot were gone from around the ground-floor windows. All that remained of the tragedy — for it was one, it was learned that it had been a deliberate act of vengeance by a teenager forbidden to see her boyfriend — was the ongoing traffic of service vehicles: cleaners, carpenters, carpet layers, electricians. The young girl, whom Gabrielle couldn't recall having met on the street where people got around mainly by car, would disappear after having existed for a moment, the responsibility now of social services, as it happens the realm of an excellent minister.

Still, the weather was waxen all around, despite the sun that had been very active on the roofs of Montreal since dawn. It was as if it was unable to cross the river, bluish like old veins and dozing now before it had even taken notice of the day. A fine dust had settled onto the balcony furniture, Gabrielle had had to close all the windows to protect herself from it, and she'd had to eat breakfast in her kitchen. When Pierre burst in around ten o'clock, despite the air conditioning it was as if one were breathing inside an enclosure and Gabrielle had no desire for him or his work or anything else.

He'd gone prowling around the area of the fire, as she'd have done too at his age, no doubt. He brought back the first bits of news.

"Apparently she's pregnant and the guy wanted to marry her."

"So what was the problem?"

"He's Pakistani or Jamaican, nobody knows which, and the girl's parents didn't want to know, apparently they even forced her to have an abortion."

"Nice people."

Pierre poured the coffee. He was starting to take root.

"I know where they're coming from. My mother was always telling me she should have got rid of me because I was the result of some Italian passing through and she'd loved him, which wasn't a good recipe for making a kid. Now it's killing her and I don't want to go back there."

Gabrielle held back her clichés. It was the longest meaningful sentence about his background that he'd uttered in the few weeks he had been coming to her place, something welled up from it that was like a threat to what she'd thought was his tranquility, there was a difference between initiating a young male and getting to know his demons.

She sent him away on the pretext that he couldn't go on painting with the windows closed, she had errands to do and would perhaps even go to a nursery in the Laurentians that specialized in ivy, where she might find a way to plant her balcony. But after he left she didn't move. She suddenly cared about the moment of which she had just robbed him. There was a story that would live only in her, on this morning of ashes. The fire at 10,009 rue des Bouleaux was opportune, it was time for it to happen, for life to start resembling what she had hoped for when she settled into this apartment, under lock and key.

She turned on her computer, went through the disorganized files on her hard disk, found the letters that she'd never sent to her lover because he would have burned them, not out of malice but because he had no safe place to keep them. In fact they weren't love letters, because at the time, she could love him with real words, when they lay down in the middle of the day and "I love you" meant absolutely that: that they were in love with one another. To write it was superfluous, though she had now and then, in short, breathless, disposable notes.

She found the one from the highway, the last one. She had written it back in Quebec City, after one of those afternoons stolen from the university by him, from the government by her, they happened then only once a month or so and sometimes the interval was as long as six or seven weeks, making her wonder if they were still lovers.

Especially as they weren't always, he couldn't bear the thought of sleazy motels where the lingering odours of other anxious couples, most of them smokers, assailed him. They would talk in the car, then, sitting close but barely touching, a caress on the neck could last an hour, awakening a commotion in her belly, it had been genuine desire, and it always comes, how amazing.

They'd had lunch in Saint-Sauveur, in what thought of itself as a bistro because of wine and blanquettes. They had not set foot inside the art gallery; now that she was the minister responsible for that sort of place, she could no longer visit them without attracting sycophants or whiners, without people tracking her reactions or counting up their acquisitions, it was the same in bookstores where she no longer even dared to buy the English women novelists that were such a fine distraction from dreary late evenings in Quebec City.

We took the highway home, it was getting late, you weren't saying much and my role was to chatter about this and that, I was charged with telling those tales that reasonable men want to hear and there's nothing more reasonable than men like you, who were no longer twenty years old when everything toppled in the land of Quebec. The day was winding down and I was too, I'd had enough of what awaited me. I was on my way to meet Jean-Charles and the limousine, a common Chevrolet full of insipid newspapers and woeful files, and he would drop me off two hours later at a hotel in Victoriaville with mauve and pink carpets where at some meeting or other I would unveil some elements of the future cultural education policy that was still gestating. At the end of the meal I would hear spoons clinking in coffee cups, the sound of the infinite lack of attention that greets our speeches and stands apart from them before they're delivered, even though these people would have taken umbrage had I refused them my presence. When at length they applaud not my words but the fact that it's time for a drink or bed, I am still thinking only of you. I call you in my head. The line crackles and burns between us who are never there.

Never weary, like this afternoon in your car — canary yellow for a daytime delinquent. It was my role to tell stories and I concocted them easily. Along highway 440, at the level of what had been Fabreville, stands a series of pink brick buildings with brown roofs, each of which holds around twenty apartments. I pointed out that you never see anyone on the balconies, even when the day is declining and the sky is turning gold, which will surprise only the simpleminded. When you settle here, into what was recently the middle of nowhere, with hay, cows and horses, the sociologist tells you that it's not so as to gawk at the horizon that's been stolen from our good farmers, or to hear the lighthearted songs of their swallows, which are well and truly gone. The place has been tamed, the doors merely open onto screens. It's inside that it is pleasant, in the unvarying light of kitchens and corridors, sheltered from nature's dirty tricks that make every species prey for another, particularly among the loveliest shadows and the softest sounds.

My presentation had conviction. I was imagining the serenity in every one of those fine and private places along the highway, because no doubt people live there who have suffered pain, whose children have betrayed them, whose villages have been destroyed by bombs in hills that are nonetheless enchanted, who have been stripped of love and even of coitus by something ugly, who have perfected arts that no one wanted. When the television murmurs and the clean sink goes pale under the fluorescent lights, they are untouchable. They achieve peace, whereas I, with my hand on your knee and knowing that I arouse you, my pleasure is too acute, filled with dread. I am already preparing to forbid myself, as always, to have the grief of you.

Then I told you the shocking story of the girl who would move there after a love affair gone sour, who would be still too young. As in Pasolini's film, she would set fire to all these tidy existences. Before long she would seduce the oldest man, fumble around in his tin trunk, that of a Balkan refugee, only to discover that he was not victim but executioner. She would open up about it to the plump sad woman, abandoned by her descendants, and be surprised to find that she too was on the side of the killers, for she was the wicked stepmother, now forgotten, the one who crammed her twins with rotten food and whose dogs were fawned upon, there had been stories in the newspapers years ago. Then she would attempt to be proven right by an ugly normal woman, one who goes shopping with coupons and cleans her length of corridor herself, to hear her say that children are poison, that she was once a schoolteacher and that the only way to survive is by constantly overcoming the temptation to torture the handsomest of the little men, those future lovers of dolls. And she would buy from the failed artist one of his youthful pieces; with hope revived, he'd go back to his dying.

What would become of this haunted house in the final sequence?

You laughed, it was obvious to you that I was seeing myself as the Pasolinian girl and that this whole hodgepodge was only the desire, a vain and stupid one, to reach some semblance of Italy instead of Victoriaville on a night that was turning to rain. You upbraided me a little for my way of going under protest to see useful people, public service is in your blood and you'd like me to be the same. What you love in me though is the very opposite of the good behaviour you've been able to teach me. It's a talent I have. When you come on my grey-hound back you defy and you dance, I'm tenderly well placed to know, it leaves marks on my corolla as they say in erotic novels from the nineteenth century, I could have been a character in one, I have their same lightness.

And so we went, crusaders, on this day when we had nonetheless barely touched. Perverse abstinence. As for those pink brick houses where people go to sleep before the sun, where they construct a kind of peace with sharp angles, where pent-up love can become tolerable, it was on that day that I began to desire them.

Sunlight slanted in, divided the parquet into yellow and grey. The computer lisped its background noise, the day would be watertight. That day, Gabrielle wrote the final instalment, it was what she was there for.

The morning I went to the Morgentaler Clinic, Madeleine came with me. We took a taxi. The fetus wasn't yours, or so we thought, but that was not the reason for your absence. You loathe hospitals, not so much because of the colour and smell as the shamelessness with which viscera, blood, excrement are treated. You are such a reserved creature.

An abortion clinic has nothing to do with that however, or very little. The curtains are brightly coloured, the reception desk is like one at an inn, the nurses wear the engaging smiles of massage therapists who presently will strip you, unembarrassed.

They took me before they opened, a small act of cowardice that had been recommended by the management secretary, to spare me the curiosity of others. Yet there was nothing scandalous, the procedure hadn't been illegal for a long time now, thanks notably to some women as well known as me who had signed petitions, declared that they'd all been there. The yellowest press couldn't have pointed to my presence at Morgentaler's without creating an immediate mobilization that would have been a rampart for me, and no one would have dared to ask a free, mature and independent woman who the father was. Still, I was grateful for the privilege of such discretion, telling myself in fact that these were things women had fought for.

The officiating physician was young and handsome, I mention that because I noticed, yes, I am frivolous. I remember an instrument at work, grey, metal, cold between my legs, it was hidden by a sky blue sheet but I could see it through the eye that we all have in our vaginas. He explained the vacuum machine to occupy my mind while he was working, and I could indeed hear the tube sucking out the waste matter he was extirpating from me and which he of course didn't show me. It wasn't too painful but he did say something very bad: "The mass is significant. You may have been pregnant longer than we estimated."

If he was right, the child was yours.

It was the accident I'd tried for months to bring on. I'd given up the IUD, I'd even bought a soft jersey dress, brick red, a designer model, which I wore too often, for the pleasure of letting my stomach become familiar with its fullness. At the slightest nausea at my desk in the National Assembly, where I often felt that way for various reasons, I would track a bubble rising from my entrails to my head, it bore your son — I never doubted that it would have been a boy, complicated like you but with dark brown eyes like mine because, according to Mendelian law, the gene for brown eyes is dominant. But the tests delivered from pharmacy to pharmacy to Madeleine, who was in on it, were always negative. My red dress, which in fact you didn't like, was sterile.

Why did I have sex with a stranger after the brief official trip to Italy that I'd extended by three days on the Adriatic for myself? I was able to tell Madeleine that the weeks had been long without you, that I was exasperated, or desperate, that finally, away from home, I had worked up the courage to anger you by taking the stupidest risk, to sneer at your intelligence, your wisdom and its laws. No, that's not true, you had nothing to do with it. The man was there for the taking, he was smooth, easy, hot, he made me laugh for forty-eight hours, took me dancing on the sand, humming his song. I have a nomadic body, I always have, you knew that too before you took me, and when I drink I can have the mind of a shop girl who sees herself whirling on the beach with a handsome dark-haired man in the setting sun.

That was why, when a nurse sat me in a deep armchair, wrapped in a warm sheet, and suggested that I rest as she stroked my hand for a moment, I whirled again. I had plenty of sobs, the kind that she, a nice girl with beautiful teeth and golden hair, would soothe again and again, all day long. Mine welled up from nowhere or from my shoulders, a little higher than my heart in any case. I saw myself as the very image of infinite desolation because a thread of blood would be soaked up by the white gauze that parted my legs, what a pity.

Madeleine brought me back to the house. My absence was shorter than for a case of bronchitis, the whole thing was uncomplicated.

You came by day after day, for a few minutes or an hour. I'd rarely seen you so often. We engaged in idle chitchat, you kept asking if I needed anything, as if chocolate or tea or a newspaper could make the late afternoons pass. The evening when you decided to rock me, with all the lights out, to murmur that I must get over the black spider dwelling in me, I thought you were about to take me back and that life would be more beautiful, because more solemn than before, like in the song about the lovers, those whose bodies are exultant yet who know that they're together in a bedroom without a cradle.

The time had come to be more beautiful than before, and under your fingers I was, you left very late, for once. And never came back.

But I am certainly more beautiful than before. There's light in my little head that has chosen to come here to be illuminated, as if it were a clinic where they kindly extirpate waste matter from you before it builds up.

What I know is that you didn't leave because of the boy on the shore of the Adriatic. At the moment when I was dancing with him, you were starting to look at other women less innocently and to acquire from me some lightness that may have led you afterwards to the bed of some laughing woman or other. Nor did you leave because of the child, that ball of shadow that disappeared at an age when it's still possible to have two fathers. You left because I'd lied to you about my desires and the reasons for the red dress, and because I made love to you with ulterior motives, with thoughts that betrayed our luminous noons and that betrayed you.

Is lying exhaustible, like grief? For two years now I've

been walking in the long labyrinth of my black spider that I'll finally arrive at, my sister, my friend, who will tell me why I was born dark and deceitful. When I hold her in the palm of my hand — she is here, I saw her yesterday, before the night — you will come back and you'll take my key. As we will be old, we'll sleep together all through the night.

While I wait I am alive and I know that you are in the city.

Thus wrote Gabrielle, in vain.

SIX

PIERRE COULDN'T HAVE cared less about Gabrielle's sudden aloofness. The beginning of August is rich with storms, Laval's malls are made for taking shelter, for stopping the wind, the rain and later on the snow, all those climates he'd hoped to escape for good when he left the North. Surprised that he'd taken months to discover their endless corridors, he never tired of walking on the cold tiles, of breathing the smell of rags that rose from the fast-food restaurants, of hearing children sniffle and fake fountains wheeze. He paid particular attention to the icy store-window dummies that didn't all resemble one another, regardless of what people think. Though window-dressing fashion dictated headless women, you could distinguish between the sylphlike and the union types from the size of their busts, the angle of the neck, the thickness of the waist, though they all lacked buttocks as did the male dummies in the neighbouring stores, which were insignificant in comparison.

Pierre turned up around noon, wolfed down some chemically fresh doughnuts from the day before washed down with a spruce beer, didn't touch the soiled and crumpled newspapers on the tables whose screaming headlines would give you a bead on this country. Lightning had killed a golfer, a former cabinet minister had drowned in his pool, the Hells Angels had acquired a historic manor house, an epidemic of caterpillars was ruining the lives of campers in the Laurentians, the explosion of the Chernobyl power station would leave thousands dead there and could contaminate the skies of Canada. But fortunately there were no skies here, where the air was purified by passing through vast wind tunnels whose rumbling could be heard behind the washrooms. Late that afternoon, after the final coffee break for young salesgirls more or less clad in rayon and polyester, whose sour speech he liked listening to, he would hang around the arcade till late at night if he happened to be at the Carrefour Laval.

The blistering hot levers on the machines created mauve and silver movements for the season's most hopeless young males. With his belly pressed against some electronic tomb where sparks made love to mermaids, to Ferraris, to gold ingots or vanishing horizons, Pierre thought more clearly about Gabrielle, about the cloying whiteness of her walls, her hips, her breasts. She was a store dummy with a head, burdened with eyes that diminished him. That wanted to take something from him. *Free game.* His cock at rest, he reddened his palms against glass and metal and discovered that he was happier.

One Wednesday around six o'clock there was a power failure. In the darkness pierced by the glimmer of exit signs, the young men tossed off curses that sounded, after so much noise, like silence. After lashing out at the flanks of some dead machines, they began to scatter. A tall man with very curly grey hair, whom Pierre hadn't noticed but who was perhaps the arcade manager, went out with them, offered cigarettes to those who were lingering around one of the entrances to the mall. An unfamiliar sun was showing through the final curtain of rain at the very back of the parking lot. The grey-haired man invited three or four of the young men to board his luxury van, a black Yukon with two rows of seats, they would go to St. Catherine Street West, power failures usually spare the downtown area and besides going to the arcades, they could spend some time in the dens of the triple-X dancers upstairs. Pierre followed him. In the spreading rosy dusk he thought the man's features were a little delicate for a connoisseur of dancers. But there was beer in the trunk, which might help him overcome his reserve and drop a few bits of sentences here and there into the string of expletives that served as the young men's reaction to the unexpected as they travelled towards adventure. On the other side of the Viau bridge, the north end of Montreal was as deserted as Laval, they spattered only the void, though there were lights on behind the blinds and fences. Even so, they shuddered a little in their damp T-shirts, as they went directly inside the Cabaret du Sexe.

They all duly went for a piss, then the grey-haired man, insisting that they call him Jérôme, flopped down next to Pierre on a sofa recently covered in leatherette. The dancers were taking a break, except one little brunette with round thighs, uncomfortable in an overly tight G-string. Facing the back of the stage she swayed her hips, spreading the cheeks of her ass with her hands, as if it were an obscene gesture. To believe that, she'd have to be a student of literature. Jérôme took a notebook from one of the big pockets of his safari shirt and began to draw. Pierre thought it was the outline of the girl but he saw that it was the profile of the brothel red lamp that only lit the arm of the sofa. Jérôme finally turned towards him.

"Your hair's a weird colour."

"Yes."

"Is it dyed?"

"No, natural."

"So your parents aren't from around here."

"Around here, somewhere else, what difference does it make to you?"

"I study men, it's what I do."

He fell silent. Three long-haired dancers, clearly well

aware of the ways of masculine concupiscence, were offering themselves in full frontal view, breasts swaying to a blues number, eyes smiling at the young men's flies and then, without actually doing anything, miming some lesbian foreplay. To really warm the place up though they'd have needed more customers. After twenty minutes, the scene ended with the propriety of an old video and the little brunette substitute came back on duty. Pierre was sure that now Jérôme was going to touch his arm or his thigh, unless instead he slipped a hand into his fawn-coloured hair, the way his mother's logger clients used to do in the last camps of the North, wrecks who would have fucked a muskrat if they could, who jerked off while they groped at the underpants of a child. Jérôme's face was blank like theirs just then, but he gave Pierre a shove and got up. "I'm hungry. Want to come to Ben's?" They left behind the others who had shed their embarrassment among themselves and now were chuckling about cunts.

Over a smoked-meat sandwich oozing orange mustard, in the most brightly lit restaurant in town, Jérôme asked his permission to take some notes on the origin of his fawn-coloured hair — a cross between the acerbic blonde of a Corrine of the miners' taverns and the mahogany mane of an Italian moaning for the sun he'd left behind. Jérôme recorded the bits that the boy dropped parsimoniously. Pierre didn't know if the ashes of his father, a suicide, had gone back to Sicily or to whom they would have been sent. He didn't know where Corrine was since she'd recycled herself as a cook in hunting and fishing camps for Americans. Surely she didn't sleep around any more but who could say? She was in her fifties now at most and would no longer be the object of such close attention from men getting drunk in the new-style lodges with their pathetic clientele of nouveaux riches. Pierre recalled Marie as being merely a temporary guardian. "She comes from up north, she's a friend of my mother's, she left her husband there, an immigrant with no ambition. She's a teacher here. And she's in mourning for her lover, a well-known man who wrote books about art." Jérôme tried briefly to learn more, but in vain. The alcohol of Laval and the cabaret had dispersed, the ceiling lights at Ben's were becoming stage lights, the coffee had cooled down at the first sip.

In the Yukon that brought Pierre back to rue des Bouleaux, Jérôme explained his vehicle and his grey notebooks through his profession — he was a retired anthropologist, now itinerant. He claimed he was collecting data on unsuccessful crosses between the peoples who meet here, in this land of immigration, whereas most of his colleagues, those who published, were more interested in demonstrating the new vitality that comes from interbreeding. Their research was better regarded and above all, better funded. A great part of the truth, and of their errors, could be seen by observing nude dancers, the most easily observable human beings, which was why Jérôme came to watch them regularly. "Remember the little brunette, the chubby one who was so self-conscious in her G-string? Just looking at her I know that her mother must be Huron or Iroquois and her father of old French stock, from a bad lineage, all of them poor half-wits. That gives you an intellect stuffed with confused connections, with some fine savage instincts but an even stronger atavistic predisposition to submissiveness. It also produces a very tough physical type, with solid flesh and short limbs. Natural survivors, yes, but confused inside their heads, with a gift for perpetual hesitation, for non-existence. It seems to me that most of our interbreeding leads to individuals like that, I call them subtractions. Other researchers, the ones who speak, see them as additions. It might be different in another country where desires may trigger passions, forge characters with those mixtures, I don't really know."

They were approaching the island of Laval. "You," Jérôme added, "you could have been a wild animal." But in profile under the suburban street lamps, Pierre resembled at most a stubborn fox, a sly little animal for whom even rabies isn't fatal in these regions. Then the man began to laugh, barely audibly. From a distance, from more than forty years, suddenly came to his ears the first notes of *Peter and the Wolf*, the Prokofiev record that had been played so often in the luxurious house of his childhood. He no longer recalled the end of the story but all at once he understood that the words of the tale, quietly recounted to the horror music, had resulted in the destruction of terror in some pampered children. From the dark forests where the wolf gorges on blood should have risen the smell of crime, the sweat and excrement of torture victims, the gas from decaying carcasses. And from that stinking mist, after the dumb death rattle of the slain, the true sound of death — that of the killer licking his chops — should have ascended. The Russian steppes still know something about that, about those dawns when the tyrant goes to bed sated while his clones aim at the cities, in their offices that stand in for watchtowers.

But what was he afraid of, this boy falling silent at his side, settled into the costly cushions, taken into streets purged of all vermin? At most, the rutting of another male, or even his mere insistence on conversing, as if prying out a few words were a form of rape. His night, which in that respect resembled the nights in all the apartment buildings lined up in their inconsequential sleep, was not weighted with any other threat, no dogs were out. Yet fear was on the prowl in the cabin.

Jérôme fed a cassette of Pergolesi's *Stabat Mater* into the tape deck, the truck was filled with the luminous voices, and Pierre had only to get out quietly, cooled down, at the door to the big pink brick cage where he was spending the summer. At least he was walking upright, his shoulders square. Jérôme had a fairly accurate idea of the mother, a bare-armed woman who surely didn't bend beneath men, the kind who would have screwed them in broad daylight. The father was a bigger puzzle. After all, he had begotten this duplicitous youth who, like so many who hung around the arcades, was lazy only when it came to thinking. The fraudulent youth could also be the wolf who's waiting for his moment. *This Peter, Pierre, is the wolf.* Jérôme promised himself that he'd track down the Prokofiev record, no doubt its stupefying version had been reissued a thousand times, and went off to his ranch in Saint-Lazare to transcribe his notes into the database that he would never submit for publication. In any event, if he were to do that he'd have had to pursue his investigation a little further.

It was midnight, that is to say very late inside the pink brick cage, when Pierre stepped inside Marie's apartment, still excited from the choral singing. The lights were all still on in the apartment, which was laid out exactly like Gabrielle's but far less carefully designed. A few pieces of antique furniture, a French-inspired armoire, a near-refectory table, two brass standing lamps with jigsawed brass bases, had been flung among square armchairs, plain carpets and a few paintings. The only works of art, prints by Francine Simonin with broad streaks, soaring or fixed in mauve and yellow, still waited to be hung. There were a few plates on the serving hatch to the kitchen, that was unusual, and the TV set was spitting out a black-and-white film that from a distance sounded like a war movie, which was not at all like Marie.

The door to her bedroom was open, in fact she never closed it. He heard her moving around. He stood in the doorway, surprised. She was filling two big suitcases that he'd never seen. One, already packed, seemed to overflow with lightweight clothing. In the other, a jumble of papers and books was piling up.

She greeted him with a preoccupied smile. "I decided to make some headway with my preparations while I waited for you. I'm leaving on Saturday for a few months." She was going overseas to teach and he could stay in the apartment, in fact she preferred to entrust it to him.

She talked to him a little about her next place, Ethiopia, as if it were the next town, while she went on bustling about. He watched her moving to the sound of gunfire from the living room. Her fine hair pulled back roughly into a ponytail, held by a blue elastic. Her fingers, almost too thin, the polish on the nails with golden accents. A red dress that fell straight, with no waist, over hips not as slim as the ass. The bare feet that maintained the arch of the high-heeled sandals she inflicted on herself all summer. The beauty spot, hairy perhaps, that marked her left cheek and held the night on her face, the face of a woman with light brown hair he had never dared to discover from up close and who would escape him.

It never crossed his mind to touch her or to push her down as he had Gabrielle. He found her strange now, suddenly distinct from the vaguely concerned and smiling figure she'd always been to him. According to his mother, who scowled as she recounted these events, Marie had wanted to abduct him when he was a child. She had coveted him, quenched his thirst with the finest milks and soothed his fever, and Corrine had had to go away to disengage Pierre from such unwholesome suffocation. According to Corrine at any rate, and it didn't make much sense because in her wandering, she seemed always burdened with her son and was prompt to chuck him for hours to anyone who would take him. When he had reconnected with Marie, she'd shown no sign of coveting him, but it was true that she tended to want him better fed, to slake his thirst incessantly, to protect him from the sun. "You burn enough as it is," she would say, a remark he didn't try to understand. So the reason she'd let him wander since the beginning of summer was that she was preparing to abandon him, he guessed, and he was surprised at the capacity for lying in a woman who'd seemed unlike the others.

It was really late; she ordered him to go to sleep, in the schoolmistress-y voice that she sometimes used and that he'd be glad to get away from.

The next two days were idiotic. She had to arrange with the bank to issue drafts for the mortgage payments in her absence, get the long list of over-the-counter drugs and sunscreens she assumed she wouldn't find in Ethiopia, fill out medical insurance forms in the event of accident or repatriation, meet the nervous beginner who would replace her in a class of the emotionally challenged in the fall, and make sure that Pierre was registered in a nearby college where she'd managed to have him admitted despite his borderline grades. There was also Fatima to be mollified, who had, in her other language but quite clearly, cursed the news that this trouble-free occupant was going away and that a teenager who she sensed was filled with glowing embers would be camping in her stead.

Pierre had at least instinctively grasped the way to cooperate. With Virginia, he established the peace of orphans. He took her to the corner store for ice cream while the women talked, and he spoke American to her, repeating the syllables of the summer's hit parade. He understood practically nothing of the words in these songs about excited bodies, about swelling sex, and Virginia was too young to go there. Besides, without music Pierre had the wrong accent and knew even less what he was saying. It was Thursday. The next day, Virginia was still clinging to his legs when he helped Fatima bring in the garbage cans, as Marie had suggested, and near the fence at the water's edge he gave her a silent botany lesson. On a few square centimetres of lawn he showed her ten kinds of weeds and even more, the pleasure to be had from pulling them, digging to the root with a fingernail, through the damp-crusted dusty surface where the grass clung, from which it drew its yellow-green by sucking up the black. The little girl's laugh was shrill and long as she scraped at the soil with fingers already darkened.

Strange that Fatima should leave her with this boy who could have abused her, there was abundant talk about such things in the cities, about the threats against little girls who were regularly found deflowered, their throats slit, always in the vicinity of water, because Montreal is an island, with countless creeks in its suburbs for committing evil.

On Saturday, Marie's departure was set for 7:40 p.m., like most transatlantic flights. She would stop over in Frankfurt, then leave at dawn for Addis Ababa, there wasn't even one full day of transit between rue des Bouleaux and the Hilton where all foreigners who were interested in their safety stayed.

Pierre was surprised that Marie wanted him at the airport, true, he was the person closest to her, of her women friends he only knew a few and they were married, abstracted, casual. It was also true that her suitcases were heavy. He felt very sure of himself as he drove the Ford Capri, an old fake sports model that she was fond of and was leaving with him for its last few usable months. He liked the corridors at Mirabel, packed with people, yet deserted. He found a thousand shades of grey there, crossed by the yellow plastic counters that took away any urge to cry. The restaurants, constantly being remodelled, sputtered with the sounds of work and gave off no odour. Yet beneath the high ceilings there was something like pure air that could go to your head. Freedom without the skies, it can exist.

For the first time in three days, Marie talked about her destination. She was going to train teachers who would go on to train others in that vast country with its hundreds of ethnic groups, its fifty million humans, to which it had taken war to bring a handful of roads but where schools were plentiful, more so than anywhere else in Africa. Since the dawn of time they had been a people of books, but there were concerns that only the culture inherited from parchment was being handed down, now they must add English and the training of masters with an aptitude for teaching it. Her knowledge of English was good, coming as she did from a border region where you couldn't survive without first hearing, then speaking it. She had even now and then escaped entirely into that language, where dreams were without depth or danger.

And then, Ethiopia was Abyssinia. She had always assured her lover, the François who had died and whom she wanted to convince of her ability to live without him, that it was her own, Marie's, desire to make her way to Abyssinia. He mocked her, did François, he didn't believe her, he'd come across so many poets whose impotence festered on the routes that Rimbaud had taken, he warned her about all the pilgrimage clichés. But Rimbaud had nothing to do with this journey, which had started thirty years before with a children's book she had later lost. It was about King Solomon and the Queen of Sheba, shown in an illustration lying under a tree whose name seemed familiar to her.

"From Abitibi to Abyssinia," she concluded as she swallowed the last sip of bad cappuccino. The scenario was stupid but according to her, the absurd was an interesting bulwark against the temptations of misfortune, which for some time had been brushing against her.

He thought he understood and so became mature. Framed by sleigh bells, the voice of Noël-Christmas announcing departures had just summoned the Air Canada passengers en route to Frankfurt. Near the frosted wall that concealed the security control, they were supposed to kiss. They embraced. He was a head taller and could press her whole body against his, from shoulder blade to thighs. He had a violent erection against Marie's belly. He stirred her, she caught fire, he'd done it. On his own he pulled away, her back was already turned. He was free now, and angry.

SEVEN

THE BLOND LABRADOR that belongs to the Canadian ambassador to Ethiopia, the Sudan and Somalia, is panting, flopped beside the indoor fountain that gives the fortified residence an unexpected grace. Between Oscar's paws rolls a grey bone, normally forbidden on the straw carpet that matches so well the light that has finally come back to the late-September sky after a more than usually vicious monsoon. But Oscar's mistress and the children are on holiday with her family in Jonquière — statutory advantage in a posting classified as difficult. In front of the tablecloth that would be immaculate were it not for the trace of blueberry coulis on angel food cake he's just been served, the diplomat lights a cigarette, it's allowed in the garden.

He thinks he can recall the still-young woman who will occupy his entire afternoon at the chancery. Her personal effects have to be sorted, by his secretary as much as possible, it's more discreet to have another woman deal with what might be intimate objects. Communicate with Ottawa about repatriating the body and most important, find out how to get in touch with her family. Who knows if the satellite phone will be working today? And more, who knows if she even has a family? Because if she was the aid worker in a red dress that fell straight over her hips but was slit fairly high on her left thigh — he has served under a dozen sunny latitudes and flatters himself that he can spot the thousand ways of baring flesh — a woman he met at the home of his American counterpart at the beginning of the month, this will be a difficult case.

He who so loved the country, to the point of staying

behind when his family fled to Quebec during the summer rainy season, had exaggerated its baleful effects, to warn her. Of course he understood her boredom with Addis Ababa, a city that was dead day and night by order of the tyrant whose sinister image dominated public places, guarded by henchmen in Mao-collared grey jackets. She'd had enough of the Hilton's discos where the international famine workers took turns having a short break from the shorn land in the north, from the hospitals where they saw children about to die, unable even to swallow, from the tents where they saw others being born, deformed for life, from the adult eyes burned by humiliation that no water could wash away, and from the rumbling of war, booming, sated, through this decay. Evenings, they savoured fresh pasta at the Italian restaurant downtown, going there in procession for fear of more or less recognized cutthroats, or made do with the hotel's American meals before getting together with the gorgeous prostitutes tolerated by the regime, the most beautiful Semites on earth. For foreign currency, these women were prepared to embrace any of the awkward bighearted leftists recruited on other continents by their churches, most of them Protestant and prudish.

It wouldn't be the first time, he'd told the woman with the insolent eyes, that young men would lose their innocence during a journey of sanctification, he'd known many of his own generation who had left their virginity behind at *Jeunesse étudiante catholique* summer camps. But she showed no interest in observing such an ordinary phenomenon and she was weary of her vain searches in Addis for some cultural signs of the ancient land for which she'd prepared herself. The tyrant had purged the city, muzzled historians and musicians, even banished embroidered cottons from the markets where local crafts had been replaced by plastic utensils imported from China. She was not a famine worker, she was part of a pilot teacher-training project set up by CARE USA, tolerated for reasons of currency and the need, even in a communist country, to master international English, the kind that was heard around the oh-so-prosperous hotel pool and tennis court. Some new form of extortion or some whim on the part of the men in grey had postponed the start of the CARE program till the beginning of October, and she wanted to get out of Addis, something the ambassador had strongly advised against, even if what she had in mind was mainly the Abyssinian plateaus, which war and famine had spared. The entire territory was nevertheless crisscrossed by foreigners in the pay of the tyrant's allies, or spies in the service of his enemies in nearby Eritrea, he had told her, and everywhere, the poverty was so sordid that the safety of tourists could not be guaranteed, not even among a people recognized for their integrity and gentleness. In the rare villages petty gangsters were now beginning to lay down the law.

He had also brought up the question of spoiled meat from diseased herds, of schistosomiasis in the ponds and lakes, and above all of the dangers during the final days of the monsoon, when you think you're settled into the dry season and then the downpour comes out of nowhere, transforming the rocky paths into swamps, blurring all markers. To reach the high plateaus then, crossing the gorges became a nightmare, he himself had had to retrace his steps last year at an even later date, it was madness to venture there, even if the terrible drought in the north seemed to alleviate the rain in the centre of the country.

It wasn't normal for her to have listened to him so abstractedly, the two of them compatriots happy to meet here surrounded by American murmurs, saved briefly from the boredom of ambassadorial salons, which were particularly beige in Ethiopia because any traditional object found locally, which were generally prized by foreign decorators, was prohibited in deference to the moods of the regime. She didn't care about risks, she said. At the suggestion of the Italian restaurant owner in Addis, she had hired for a high price an experienced Ethiopian driver, whose huge Jeep could generally get out of any unsuspected dangers. "And if I disappear, don't go looking for me. There's no one to claim my remains." She was smiling, playing the confident loner, but he was convinced of her incompetence. He had met a good many intrepid souls with no apparent family ties only to discover, when they were repatriated maimed or dead, that they had fled marital problems and flocks of descendants who would fight over the insurance for years. This girl, who could have been his type if he hadn't been the contented lover of his own wife, definitely had the intelligence necessary for lying, so their conversation was in fact inconsequential.

And now here he has close at hand, in writing that reminds him of his mother — whose letters he'd read and loved across all the distances from which she had written him over a period of more than twenty years — the journal found in the bag of a dead woman who may be, who is without a doubt, the woman in red from the American salon. According to the Ethiopian soldiers' report, the accident had occurred two days earlier, during the terrible descent from Dejem, the one that plunges towards the shoddy bridge over the blue Nile. She'd been on her way home then, a day at most from the capital. But it was only yesterday that the sky had finally cleared.

He suppresses a temptation to go to Dejem, has a memory of green tea, its taste masked by the smell of turpentine that permeated the inn and its overly high walls, erected against unlikely inquisitors. Last year he'd spent a night in that village, a stopping place, which was perched as a belvedere above the canyon, with its long houses, pride of the rich, built to last, yet more humid than the huts made of cow dung that were scattered over the far-away plateaus. It had been a true African night, solitary, filled with obsessive fears and ghosts that refuse to disperse before dawn, that enter blindly the mauve of regret, pummelling what have to be called sins, irreparable debris of a life spent drinking, eating, smoking, caressing, talking — while waiting to accomplish great things. Some of those magnificent things of which one could see the yellowing underside, in the distance near Sudan, the last ray of light in a dusk that would not retreat.

What would be the point? He knows what she saw when she was dying and that it bears no resemblance to Dejem's diffident luxuriance. The accident must have happened in the afternoon, drivers usually stop before nightfall. But when it rains, even in broad daylight the descent is a night. And it brings to bear on travellers the most powerful of seductions — the appeal of melancholy. Spread out like huge recumbent images, the plains at the summit lose their few areolas in the fine shades of grey of the sky, the breath of clouds brushes against the skins of animals and earth, the sharpness of the cliffs becomes a sooty fleece that it would be good to sink into. Vertigo, the body's rudimentary caution, vanishes. What's a little silt on the road? The foam of this sea of sky, of which one must touch the bottom. In that way the sun, when it becomes visible again during the descent from Dejem, regularly finds shattered men to burn who in reality are drowned.

Today, the tribute is a woman, a more uncommon event

in these escarpments transformed into a cemetery of all the carcasses, carts, Jeeps, buses, and tractor-trailers, whose young drivers are sometimes spared, they fling themselves onto the road as soon as they lose control of the wheel and let their load go hurtling down, plunging kilometres further along and catching fire. Their iron sun crackles in silence, from the belvedere, villagers will look down on it. They stopped counting some time ago.

The first to arrive at the scene of the minor carnage of a Jeep with driver and passenger will have been the children of course, as agile on the mountain peaks as their goats. Two boys and a girl, shivering at dawn in the frayed blankets that enveloped them from knees to head, their fingers as fine as their features, inherited from Araby, the eyes without fear because they're unacquainted with mirrors. If they touched the dead women in red, or in blue denim because probably she hadn't travelled in her dress, it will have been the way they approach any foreigner, gripping her hand as a sign of friendship for these lost souls whose concern or even sorrow they can guess at, they're confronted with so much space and horizon. They won't have stolen anything, they take only what they are given. Even the youngest ones, in robes the colour of their sheep, have that reserve. Afterwards they'll have crouched down, unmoving, guardians of the blue, empty sky, till an implacable sun rises at noon and their older brothers arrive, whose work is to convey stones from the mountains, who are able to transport corpses too. Still hesitant, the blue sky will then have cast a green glow over the mass of fallen rocks, as if moss were dancing where the children pass. The Jeep will have impaled itself halfway there, still a long way from the bed of the Nile, replete and brown, on the season's rich alluvium. If she bled to death and sensed for a moment the iridescence of dawn, at least

Abyssinia will have spared her its lot of dirt. She hadn't got to the bridge, which is under surveillance by soldiers in boots and berets, sentinels in decrepit shacks, wary-eyed and rifles at the ready. They would have stopped her in the stifling heat that makes them so malevolent deep down in the canyon, and they would have been odious for hours. Instead of that she had rested for a moment in the light, when her pain had departed before life itself.

The Canadian ambassador to Ethiopia, who is also responsible for Sudan and Somalia, has a most poetic way of toning down the probable terror of one of his nationals, who's been stolen from her family and friends by a terrible accident on the way out of Gojam province on a day of impenetrable fog. But he won't share his ranting with the woman's relatives and he wonders why he's so impressed by the incident, he has known worse: two teenagers whose throats were cut in the middle of the old Roman road outside Algiers, an archaeologist held and tortured by thieves in an abandoned grotto in Petra, a colleague shot to death in a Cairo souk. That the most recent Abyssinian rains should take a life is normal, they've always done so at the end of the season, just as the ice in Quebec's rivers claims its victims every spring.

He can't help feeling though that this woman wanted the descent from Dejem to be a journey with no return.

He pulls himself together, accuses himself of suffering from the "colonial blues" of which Michel Leiris, the literary ethnologist, wrote in *L'Afrique fantôme*, an account of the minor woes encountered by a 1933 mission from France during the famous crossing from Dakar to Djibouti. The ambassador is one of the very few to have read and savoured every page. The distinguished Leiris, who spent as much time bickering with camel drivers and wondering about his sexual abstinence as he did noting facts about African life, wrote outlines of novels he never completed. The finest is the one about the gentleman, also an ethnologist, who wants to cure himself of his impotence by sleeping with a native woman, and finally sends her away after lacerating her; then comes an epidemic that he manages to use for his own suicide, after putting all his papers in order and writing, in the form of allusions, some farewells and confessions to a distant lover. The ambassador has often dreamed of taking up this thread of Leiris's, of writing the story, bitter and nonchalant and African, of an individual so gifted for the incomplete.

Another great achievement left in the lurch. All he has written, from one difficult posting to the next, are confidential and succinct reports to ministers that were summarized by other colleagues before being filed away forever. The grey notebooks in which the woman named Marie scribbled a few pages, he's very familiar with, a good many diplomats fill similar ones instead of drinking during countless idle evenings, hoping one day to publish their memoirs, at their own expense if need be. Some do it and then turn to alcohol, retirement is sad if it's lived alongside boxes of unsold books.

Marie's squared-paper notebook, made in France by Chatelles for schoolchildren, has heavy extra-white paper and a photo of a virile Greek mask seen in profile. It's unlikely that she bought it for the picture, which has nothing to do with her. But it's well made, spiral-bound, in a size convenient for travel. Does the ambassador have the right to read it? The question is superfluous, he's alone with Oscar and why bother mastering discretion, first requirement of his profession, if it's not so as to become judiciously involved in other people's business? He pours himself a Scotch, it won't hurt just this once, and settles himself in the study, dark with bookcases, which is most often used as a TV room. He'll go back to the chancery a little later than usual, they can get along without him for a while.

First he leafs through the notebook, curious about the writing, rather untidy for a teacher, slanting sometimes left, sometimes right, with no apparent hesitation but concerned about legibility. Of a page where all the lines are used, you could say that it's reminiscent of a badly weeded lawn. But then if you look carefully it's not a diary, there are no dates, no place names, the pages follow one after the other, front and back, like the manuscript of a novel written in prison, saving paper. Yet she has filled only a quarter of the notebook, indicating that she was interrupted. Maybe, contrary to his assumption, she was not intending to die.

The first paragraph gives some indication. At the top of the page, capital letters written in blue ink by an awkward hand, read BURTUKAN, followed in parentheses by the word "orange," scribbled hastily.

Someday I'd like to revisit Burtukan, the name means orange in Amharic. Yesterday saw me at the Gennete Maryam church, the paradise of Mary, just outside the holy city of Lalibela. A surrounding wall carved out of the rock like the church held a dozen children who'd come running as soon as we arrived, one was a little girl in braids, only slightly less timid than the others. At first all I could see was her sloppily woven empire-waisted grey dress, draped as gracefully as taffeta, which grazed her ankles. She wore colourless leatherette ballerina slippers, a reject from some international charity but perfect on her feet. She said: "My name is Burtukan *[I hear Brutkan, brute, I'm stunned to hear English]*. I have a nice name. I am ten years old. What is your name?"

"Marie."

"You have a nice name, Maryam, Mary. Do you have a pen? I am in fifth grade."

She spoke with the same accent as the pupils in the first class assigned to me in Montreal when, though I hadn't really mastered it myself, I was teaching English to bored teenage girls who nonetheless pronounced it better than their own language. Over her shoulder she had a threadbare cloth bag, buttoned shut. She opened it, showed off her exercise books written in Amharic, there were crosses here and there. There was even one drawn on the back of her hand. Salomon, the driver, says that she'll be given away in marriage in two or three years, in spite of school, it's the practice outside the towns, and all Ethiopia is outside the towns. "They're so young that their first pregnancy often kills them," he noted in a voice that now sounded urban. I asked her to write her name on the first page of my notebook. Salomon said that it means "orange," an ultrarare fruit for these children, it's possible they've never tasted or even seen one. I told her in turn, "You have a nice name," and gave her my pen. I was the perfect tourist, stirred by the first of what would be, as soon as the next day, a whole series of graceful children who would materialize whenever we stopped to look at churches, trees and rocks, knowing how to declare their names in English, to request mine and to ask for pencils. At Addis, a famine worker told me that in Mekelle, the most skeletal of the children ask first for pencils from foreigners who are there to distribute milk.

But the image of Burtukan disturbs me for other reasons. As if with her notebooks, her stench of school, the iron cross around her neck, her sycophantic English, her gentle submissiveness, she were the replica of what I once was, Marie the ready-made, already false. She is the contradiction of what I've come here to look for.

The reflection stops there and the text begins again after two blank pages, as if the writer had wanted to set aside some space she could come back to during her journey, when she would have a better grasp of the nature of little Abyssinian girls. The ambassador thinks though that she has understood everything from the outset.

EIGHT

ABOVE ALL, leave Rimbaud out of it.

He has nothing to do with what I'm looking for here — that mama's boy who left home to come down with his fevers in Africa so he'd seem more interesting when it was time to meet his maker as so many others did in that era of infections and poor hygiene. He got it — his parent's pity, his sister's grief, and the everlasting veneration of those in our lands who saw themselves as damned and dangerous poets, not all of whom were lucky enough to have buggered Verlaine at the dawn of their versifying careers. Let him keep them all for his cult, those vaccinated tourists on pilgrimage to Harar with their filter-ground coffee, their tamed hyenas, their recreated Rimbo House. I too have had my Disney and Eiffel Tower periods. But at least I had the excuse of having studied literature with the nuns and of having encountered Rimbaud and Verlaine, both text and sex foreshortened, only in the Calvet textbook.

I am searching for the earthly paradise. Paradise on earth. The land of paradise. Once I'm there I myself will drive myself out. For I'm not seeking it so I can settle in, chew khat and let myself be penetrated, through the toes, by the faith of their churches you must enter in bare feet. For a moment or less, I want to see the earthly paradise without humanity inside. That's all.

It's an idea that came to me small and then grew, the way ideas do when there is still so much room in the brain. I myself had a lot when I wakened at the age of eleven, knowing very well how to read and write the trifles it was considered essential to fill my head with, in a green clapboard house with a huge willow behind it that didn't weep but that could have had reasons to do so in the area around the lane separating those who were poor and clean from the ones who were soiled. In the cellar that had a dirt floor at the time and smelled of cat pee, just next to the furnace a rock showed through, so big and solid that it had to be left in place when the basement was finished because it would have been impossible to dynamite it without endangering our big family home. I think that was where my idea came from, from the light bulb that long hung above the rock, the eye was in the grave and was looking at Cain, I suppose, but I certainly didn't make the connection at the time.

One thing is certain, nothing would suggest to me, not even in the most subliminal manner, any historical episodes prior to the one involving Cain. My parents seemed to have well and truly chosen to move as far as possible from the pleasant valley of the St. Lawrence and the indescribable charms of the lovely city of Quebec where they had met and chastely converged — I don't say "loved," how could I know that when at the time I was acquainted with them they were no longer making babies and their bedroom in the morning smelled more of mustiness than of coitus interruptus. For that matter, I couldn't have told one from the other, I didn't even know that my brothers peed from the end of a rod. Perhaps they loved one another in their way, she glad to have found someone to help her avoid the desires she dared not have, he amazed to be in the company of that pretty brunette, very temperate but industrious, at his still fairly lean side.

There was no question then of exile, never did I sense in them the slightest nostalgia for the people and things of which the bards then beginning to crisscross Quebec were declaring the sublime neo-French beauty. Cap Diamant, the Île d'Orléans, the giants who had slept there and who apparently were waking now to prepare for independence — the entire past strand of a present that was becoming glorious seemed to have left them indifferent. And even less was it a question of a sin having led to banishment. They and their friends along the St. Lawrence had inscribed on their brows the serenity of the innocent. They were careful not to sound off too much against sinners, my mother so feared carnal knowledge that even a reference to it for the purpose of condemnation struck her as perilous. With every fibre of my being, which derives from theirs for better and even more for worse, I'm certain that they hadn't tripped up before marriage.

Anyway, the forbidden fruit didn't tempt me. We ate apples very rarely, they came from Ontario by train, there were brown spots on their skin, anyone who likes that fruit is foreign to me, they make me want to vomit. Consequently, the metaphor of the apple eaten by the couple — invented to symbolize the cunnilingus and fellatio Adam and Eve discovered with delight — could have launched me on the trail of an ordeal of metaphysical dimensions, the deprivation of orgasm because of an urge to puke springs from prohibitions all religions have invented. But I wasn't really philosophical, at home we didn't have even a hint of a conversation that might have forged a link between the taste of the fruit and the meaning of life.

I have a clearer memory of garter snakes, descendants of the Serpent. They were all over, zigzagging through the patches of wild blueberries. They're short, garter snakes, and so small that you can't even see their venomless sting. They are their ancestors' lovely bastards, able to wrap themselves around an oak, they have adapted, they live in groves of aspen born from the ruins of burned spruce forests. They are exactly the colour of the peacocks in Mexico, but that's not well known because they are reluctant to let themselves be seen in the sun. If I wasn't with my sister, who would cry out at the sight of one, I was sometimes able to observe them. I spied one that was writhing on some moss, in pleasure or agony. How I envied it! I have retained of it at most some suggestion in my belly that came back to me, like the glimmer of a lightbulb, at the point when I was becoming interested in the earthly paradise that it took me a long time however to locate.

Through I know not what penchant for contradiction, something a number of those educated by the nuns are familiar with, I preferred Cain to his brother, Abel, though the pages of the Old Testament attribute to him, with no extenuating circumstances, all the miseries of the world through the ages. Today, thanks to the bits and pieces of psychology I've studied, it's easier for me to grasp the mechanisms of my adolescent reasoning. Then, I was only recently pubescent but I was one of those who were bleak, small, shy, with the creases of my childish folds inadequately smoothed. In class I rubbed shoulders with a few girls who were rich and beautiful, tall and cheerful, whose appearance matched, feature by feature, the heroines in the sagas in the *Veillées des chaumières*, those magazines for silly girls of which some French publisher dumped his surplus in the log cabins of Canada. It was obvious, clear, unquestionable that had an Abel existed, he would have been reserved for those girls, because he'd have had every virtue and a boy who has every virtue doesn't need to go fishing among the bleak to find love. He only has to choose the nicest one from the sirens placed at his disposal by their wealthy and pleasing parents. And some of them are nice, despite the reputation they've acquired for being idiots.

Unattainable, impossible — the Abels become abhorrent to girls with no assets. Cain, on the other hand, might well exist in their lives. Not only has he too been tested by envy, but also his murderer's destiny is more interesting than that of the handsome murder victim, and a girl who's in the mood to complicate her life can find reasons to slip away with him. The virtuous, for example, will want to accompany him along the road to repentance, while the depraved couldn't imagine a better accomplice in perdition. At the start of my menses I certainly didn't go that far in my calculations of destiny, but Cain was a brother to me, I attributed to him brown eyes and dark clothes whereas the other one, with his blind grace forever petrified in the flannel of his shroud, seemed instead to be a brother to the terribly tiresome Maria Goretti.

If these impressions, which should have been fleeting, have stuck in my memory, it's because I choked back several questions having to do with Cain during religion classes that were not yet catechesis so that it was impossible to discuss anything. I found it hard to understand why fratricide suffered an irreversible, eternal curse, when we were taught that every sin could be forgiven. But such questions flew away as we removed ourselves more and more from the confessionals — which in my case happened fairly early.

It was much later that the character of Cain came back to me. I was about eighteen, I'd stopped growing, I found little to do, little to think about, textbooks were still censored. Spring had been dry, inflammable, hard to live through. The town talked with stupor about a Ukrainian couple who'd taken their own lives in a shack below Nor-métal. They had been found in one another's arms beneath the black cross of the temperance movement, though they had only polluted water to drink and nothing at all to eat. My father knew them, he knew all the destitute people who tried to cultivate the Abitibi soil, he loved animals and stood in for the veterinarian with them; it was his form of proselytism, he sometimes saved the lives of calves and, to his great joy, a few horses. He'd gone to see the Ukrainians a few months earlier, but their hens had died anyway. He was not surprised by the tragedy. He came out with a few words of anger, quickly suppressed by the good Catholic he was, at the politicians and priests who deluded the workers in the cities about the fertility of the Abitibi soil. "One of the worst of the pieces of land God gave to Cain," he said about that of the Kowalchuks.

He meant by that soil that was rocky. We knew about those plots of land shaved out of areas that already were producing stunted trees. Neither machine nor man could smooth it, for the clay soil, once turned over, yielded only stones. We drove past their unfenced fields, they would have served no purpose, the animals couldn't survive on the sparse grass, dotted here and there with brown clumps of earth that towards the end of summer took on a mineral hue. As most of this land had been quickly abandoned, at best it roused amazement at the malevolence of whoever had even suggested it could be cultivated — and pity for those who'd believed it.

At an age when we want to make names for ourselves I had acquired some affection for these places. I thought they were poetic in the moonlight. The stones, turning to marble, evoked beneath our skies the sepulchral blue so prized by the Romantic poets, at least in the excerpts we were offered at the convent which was, by definition, a friend of graveyards. I savoured their silvery glints. As it had not provided food, the cultivation of mineral soil did give rise to progress in housing. Many were the small tarpaper shacks that little by little were faced with round rocks, patiently cemented. It took time, sometimes years — not for lack of material, but because once the process was started, it had to go on, using stones that were all same size, which became more laborious to collect once the surroundings had been skimmed. Long snubbed by the bourgeois whose taste extended only to cut stone, these structures are now greatly appreciated by lovers of folk art, they see them as an ingenious, aesthetic and functional way to make the most of a hostile environment. I was still far from able to formulate such judgements, but those houses seemed to me filled with joy, erected to amuse the always large numbers of children around them. The fathers of these youngsters had to have been good to have embarked on such an adventure. These houses were also the first to be graced with a few boxes of flowers, the growing of which was a luxury if not a scandal in our land that was unsuited even to vegetable gardens.

I also liked rocks for themselves. You could find them here and there in the clearings, vast and warm, where I'd go during my walks on the outskirts of town. From those shapes hollowed out by the millennia, I made for myself beds where I could close my eyes in the sun and feel my lids become iridescent, or read, silly things generally, but so what. Without shelter, skin roughened, gaze bleached, I too was a stone. I recognized myself in the area around the mines, I thought I could make out their subsoil with its veins that resembled my own, I liked hearing about the fires that would denude our landscapes even more.

When people cursed these landscapes, calling them "the land God gave to Cain," I was offended. It was entirely possible that the Ukrainian couple had committed suicide for some other reason than poverty and hunger, they could have succumbed to a longing for their native land, to a problem of sterility, to an incurable disease that would separate them and their love couldn't bear the prospect. I was still rather marked by the literary excesses of the previous century that would live on in isolated corners of French Quebec, so late to produce its own novels.

All the same, the image stuck in my mind and I found myself thinking, for the first time in a somewhat orderly manner, about Cain. I had some recollection of his crime, cutting the throat of his brother Abel to take his property, or out of jealousy over Adam and Eve's obvious preference for their eldest, an odd thing because in Quebec the youngest child is usually the best loved. The punishment though I couldn't recall, only the part about the eye that pursued him even to the grave, an allegory thoroughly exploited in our classrooms to keep us quiet when the teacher left for a few moments, entrusting us to a Cyclopean and vengeful God.

There was no question of Cain's being sentenced to prison, prisons didn't exist when there was only one family of four on earth, he too must have been banished, like his parents. An interesting notion, releasing the guilty to the four winds, returning them to wild countryside that they must tame in order to survive, instead of shutting them up and turning them into imbeciles by subjugating them. Had it not been for the unforgiving Eye, Cain would one day have become a free man. Some of his descendants think it did happen, that he divested himself of the burden of evil by cultivating his solitude, where there is no room for jealousy. In that case, in the twilight of his life the Eye would have been merely a sun that was setting and then had set. Justice and hope are better served by this thesis but when my father, who owed his education to tradition, evoked the land God gave to Cain, it seemed murderous and merciless. Not a bird passed there, not even to fly over.

And so the land where I was born, and the rock that gave me some idea of happiness by transforming me into stone, were the reproduction of cursed places. Ugly until the end of the world in the eyes of the deity and of man. Instead of being disconsolate, I surprised myself by marvelling at it. In fact it was difficult at age eighteen to hold on suddenly to a better dissidence to be explored. Cain would be my hero. I would put myself on his trail.

Here the text breaks off and a very large question mark, redrawn again and again until it cuts through the paper, seems to have been an attempt to disavow the preceding pages, as the following suggests:

But who am I so vain as to think I am, all of a sudden? A Maryam on whom an annunciation falls? No more than Burtukan, who may become her village schoolteacher, was I able to imagine any connection between the origin of the world and the land where I had grown. The story of Cain barely takes shape in my aging head, where books have talked about other books. I am scribbling on the terrace of a hotel in Lalibela that's at once new and decrepit, because my journey has been halted by the rain that closed the roads and I have nothing else to do. Constructing it gives shape to a life that had none, that tumbled down the way life does here, between people with small desires whom fate has caused to be born in spaces too big for them.

I was unaware in fact that I was on the side of Cain.

No matter what was written about it by all those men seeking to endow their Quebec with the genes of giants, even as they were settling in the most impossible places, our line has always originated in unadventurous bodies. They had certainly been hard at work, they'd opened clay roads and cleared jungles of ice, but at the end of their days, they had never stopped telling one another thin stories wherein victories were so many stakes to block their horizons: the arrival of a *caisse populaire* or a movie theatre, the passage of a surveyor, the replacement of wooden sidewalks, the building of a hospital. When they had triumphed over the elements enough to tame them, to set limits to their living and their dying, they were content — much more so than those who ventured to the poles, whose desires had no end.

I was born long after the limits were established, they had multiplied, now you need a bus to get from one to the other. And under those conditions, what was most certain was not revolt — that was something we'd have had to draw from our ancestry which was devoid of it — but boredom. It doesn't always lead to fantasies. There's an unwitting shadow over days that are nonetheless full. I don't remember having wallowed in it but I see myself coming and going in the town, checking new arrivals at two or three boutiques, making dresses and buying a coat, teaching, cashing my paycheque, phoning one woman or another about a Saturday outing, but there were six other nights in the weeks and where was I? In front of the television and sometimes in books whose titles I can't recall, past the age for novels about romance. Yet I read a lot, till late at night. And so the days, though boring from end to end, seemed short to me.

The first Cain to block my path was Ervant. I was right to leave him shortly after I'd married him because he ended up driving in even more stakes than my parents; but I rediscover, still intact, the hunger that came to me from that skittish body, that knew how to get in tune with mine so I felt constantly naked, and wet, and ready to fling myself into him again and again. I had no self-control. Today it's easy to give him the face of the outsider, the alien who disturbed villages, who seduced virgins and reduced their parents to not very much. It corresponds to the idea that we form of spasms in quiet places, they're always due to a young man who has come from some-where else, with stiff prick and mystery in his eyes. But Ervant didn't come from some Sodom, not at all, sulphur was not his country. He had fled the smell of it, which still lingered in Eastern Europe, he made love with knowledge gained in the old, self-confident cities he'd passed through without really seeing, eager to get to the New World and finding himself now and then having to assuage himself with liberated women who demanded caresses in the right places. Along the way, he had become a handsome beast.

With my appetite aroused I cared little about the futures he described to me in broken French. He would have liked to have found grace with my mother, who cold-shouldered him because he was an immigrant; dusk made him talk about big warm houses for bringing up children, he saved his money, and while he deplored them, at my insistence he recounted a few stories of women and girls on the shores of a Danube forgotten by him. I never tired of his evocations of Fatima, the little girl who'd masturbated him in a church and already knew how to demand money, it was a long way from my childhood with its odour of purity and its clean cotton undershirt.

On rue des Bouleaux the concierge is also called Fatima, she's the right age to have aroused Ervant in Vienna, and seems to me also to have the sheep's eyes that still made him blink from embarrassment and guilt when he talked about her. She would be completely square, that Fatima, without the fat deposits swelling bust and buttocks, but in her voice, in her Spanish throat, I hear the swelling that comes to little girls at the same time as the swelling of their breasts, the sound of the first fondling. If I go back there I'll try to find out if she once lived in Vienna, with a father who ran a café.

There was nothing of Cain about Ervant but his wandering, and that was coming to an end. I realized that during the year of our marriage when I befriended a woman who was more of a wanderer than him, she was hotheaded, she loved sex, she took away any desire I might have had for a child by giving birth to an acid and awkward boy, most of all she taught me the need to go away, she did so constantly. Anyway, the town was about to close in around its ultimate limits. Then came college, university, libraries, theatre, all institutions that lead us to think we are appeased. I got away from him just in time, without realizing it, mainly I had the impression that I was leaving my husband.

To become alienated as I am now, it's necessary to have been free. I had a gift for that, I think. The years before François I see as smooth and full and round, though to others they might seem a form of Lent. I had bought a small house near the school where I was teaching English to girls who were biding their time till they turned sixteen and could escape. Behind their peroxide bangs, the cheap lipstick smeared on their pouts, their smokers' voices, I nonetheless saw gazes I'd never met before, a sense of defiance that I approached but without fraternizing. I wouldn't have had the words to console them about incestuous brothers, violent boyfriends, drunken mothers. But I knew instinctively how to talk to them about other things, about the pleasure of being a brunette or their dreams of becoming nurses. It was as strange to them as Alberta or Catalonia, but they were grateful that I gave them some air; one girl became an optician and let her hair go back to being chestnut, by chance I found myself at her shop on Mont-Royal a few months ago, she remembered me as taller, she said. It's a sign that I was feeling good at the time.

The school kept me company, it was alive with the electricity of the now unbuttoned Quebec, teaching English was a very simple way to take note of it, I was doing it in a void and I didn't care. I was on my own, my pleasure was boundless. I would buy a newspaper that helped me understand the few bombs and the many demonstrations, I participated from afar by reading Vallières and acquiring political prints in galleries where I knew none of the long-haired leaders. In fact I went unnoticed though all in all I'd been a charming teacher. I had no regrets because I particularly liked to get on the road to the United States in spring, summer, fall, to go and while away the hours in Maine and Vermont, in antique stores or boutiques where people sold homemade jam. They were perfect conversationalists, anonymous too, and thanks to them I could get by without any others during the week.

In the winter I went at least once in search of something similar in Florida, there are plenty of interesting things to be found there off the paths beaten by bad taste. It was there that I heard *Orpheus* for the first time, in an Italian theatre reproduced in Sarasota, and it was there that I met François.

Since his death I can't tolerate music.

Who is worth the trouble of loving that way? Surely not the François Dubeau who is becoming blurred nowadays in itemized publications: professor of art history; teacher of a generation of artists; progenitor of his devotees through homosexual sex, which was what had actually brought him to power; among the first to die on the field of horror that the gay plague was for a time; and henceforth ennobled if not altogether tamed. As well — and this is something the articles and anthologies will never say — adulterer to all those aesthetic and amoral commitments that had won him the respect of his circle, for he had secret sex with a woman, in her brick house with fireplace, elegant suppers, Sauternes and chocolates savoured between the sheets, moonlight glinting off a white orchid, which he caressed. As if it were me, Marie.

No one can imagine. I found jubilation, as it says in the Magnificat, in that awkward body made spirit that brought to me, inside me, all the servile flesh that flowed into him, all the rage choked back in artists' studios, all the stammerings of those who would give voice to this still-mute country, all the slackening of muscles barely exercised yet already weakened by who knows what sadness about their art, when it becomes a mere meeting of those who make it, who are by definition ordinary. François's torment gave meaning and voluptuousness to things. I found the echo of it all day long, in the acidity of black coffee, in the eyes of a teenage girl in crisis, in the stripes of streets, in the stunned Muzak of supermarkets, in the uneven gold from my lamps, in the toneless voices on the radio, in the door to be locked against danger. But never again did I find in him whose words were laughter, the light hair, the fingers nimble for writing that could have created tales and canticles. I knew though what he refused to talk about in the ferocity of the world, I read it in his thin nape with the slightly twisted sinews, in his fear of orgasm, which passed through him as if despite himself. I felt I was on my knees when faced with such remorse. I sometimes thought I was pregnant by him, though I was unaware for as long as he was that the dried sperm on my skin was steeped in death.

I loved a condemned man, I loved a man who was damned, I know that because I'm no longer a free woman and I don't give a damn. I didn't see him die, he was in the arms of others who made a grave for him, and if he wrote me a letter as he'd promised, no one ever gave it to me.

It doesn't matter, I had a choice between two ways of lying down, that is of spending even longer at his side. It would be in Laval or in Abyssinia.

I thought for a while that I could be both of us, be François and me, and live in the unlikely place he'd once suggested, on a whim. He'd got the idea one night when we were returning from the Laurentians, sated on the cirque of lakes and mountains, silent now as we were on the verge of resuming our parallel lives, we were driving past the new apartment blocks springing up now along the highway access roads. They were all alike, unreal, with their deserted balconies, their flickering lights, and we couldn't tell if they reflected the setting sun or some lamp switched on at the beginning of a solitary evening. They were a long way from everything. "We'll live halfway between Laval's two shopping centres," said François.

"We'll only go out for food and wine, we'll be a ball of rosy pink in a square bed and our neighbours will be our world, they'll suffice." We'd turned it into a game, we had invented dozens of possible neighbours, from the worldly assassin to the bestial nonagenarian, from the incontinent diva to the piggish nun. We would have prowled around their secrets by night, for no reason, just for something to do, with no repercussions. Or to marvel at the fantastic human resistance to virtue, up to this very century that had designed these perfect cavities, intended to confine excess in all its forms.

I sold the house, moved to rue des Bouleaux and met there only ordinary people, an aloof concierge, a quarrelsome old couple, singles with forced smiles and — the one surprise — a former cabinet minister, still young, who seemed to have shut herself away to write her memoirs, as if anyone in Quebec could still be interested in the why's of our failures. I didn't see much of her, my balcony faced the Laurentians, hers faced the river, but there was a shared recognition between us, no doubt because we'd wandered one day into similar dead ends. She had been minister of cultural affairs and of course it was she who, for a time, awarded the grants that those in François's circles lived on. A tenuous bond, now abandoned.

But to whom do I intend to lie in this notebook that no one will read? Why have I been silent, or almost, up till now about the real Cain who is practically my son?

I was never really alone with François. In my house there was also that boy who has been clinging to me, has been underfoot, since his birth, the son of my friend of that summer following my marriage, a corrosive and passionate child who took away any desire for motherhood but whom I had to adopt despite myself. She, Corrine, remained a free woman, time and again she expelled him and turned him over to me, we were a made-up family, he and I, and as foreign to François as his virus-bearing lovers were to me. I cared for Pierre's fevers when he was a newborn, I took him in when he was a teenager, a russet shadow in my house where he stayed because he knew nothing else, no one else. I allowed him to roam the city, he never came in very late, he grew up slender, caustic, taciturn, skilled at doing odd jobs, and had no other goal. If I became his mother to some degree, it was because I was the right age, my friend had disappeared into one of the northlands she was fond of.

But most important, the silence between Pierre and me has the depth of the small Oedipal tragedies so common in our houses. He knows nothing about Phaedra, he's a product of our schools where this kind of tragedy is unknown and untaught on account of its great age, but that's how he sees me. I look brunette and passionate, my widow's weeds are red, it's possible that he is disturbed.

Pierre followed me to rue des Bouleaux, where else could he have gone? I don't know who it was that more or less deflowered him — man or woman, night or day — but he began prowling around me, sweet smelling and pubescent. Towards the end of the hottest days of summer, I kept my distance from that smouldering fire, I decided to abandon him the way one decides on an abortion, I imagine, knowing that you'll be left with a lump in your belly and that it could become like the eye of God, unless you find a way to puncture it.

The other way to keep François alive then was Abyssinia. So he'd know that he was free to exclude me from his worlds, I had told him that one day I would go to Ethiopia, a country that was the very contradiction of mine and that was intended for me. Certain books said that the first man had appeared there in the first rift in the earth, the oldest skeletons in history were exhumed there; where I come from too there were regularly born, along the last fault in the new world, bodies that might have considered themselves immortal, conquerors of the final frontier. The sun of Abyssinia flowed with milk and honey; the moon of Abitibi hardened gold and copper. I must go towards that contradiction. There I would lie down in a field of stones, their greys and blues similar to mine, to complete the circle, to recover the first moment in my life as a girl, a warm rock that streaks the skin of a child and makes her smile. In the distance, a brief storm. When I get there, the season of heavy rains would also be drawing to an end.

François did not believe in my Abyssinia, which was borrowed from a collection of illuminated manuscripts published by UNESCO, any more than he believed in the apartment in Laval. He went along with the game, the land of Rimbaud can count on a favourable bias on the part of artists or art historians who like to think themselves unkempt and suicidal, a state they confuse with the melancholy they have learned. His pet name for me was Vitalie, the name of the poet's mother and his sister. I was certainly less well prepared for a trip to Ethiopia than for a move to Laval, but I acted quickly in the middle of the summer, volunteer aid workers aren't so numerous during this period of famine when the corrupt regime appreciates English teachers all the more, because the language is that of international outlays. I have an iron constitution, I had no problems with the vaccinations and I didn't have to discuss my decision with anyone. Because I am alone, no matter what Pierre, to whom I've left the place, thinks.

At the airport, embracing me as is customary, he tried to brand me like a mare, his cock pressed hot against my hip, there is nothing more vulgar. In the plane though, dispelling the slight turmoil he'd provoked, I really did see the image of Cain taking shape — wandering, damned, hunted down. I more or less wondered, before I dozed off while waiting for the stopover at Frankfurt, why I so often found myself on the damaged side of individuals. And if it was even possible that I'd been born of a land God gave to Cain.

One thing is certain, and I am writing this journal to etch its reality indelibly, to imprint it: this morning, I saw the earthly paradise. For twenty or thirty minutes, I don't know which, along the road to Lalibela. We had set out early because the road might be hard to negotiate, it had rained until late the day before. But at eight o'clock, when the truck turned onto the first rocky outcropping that seemed from the beginning to block the road, the air was as dry as the stones. We were driving slowly but still stirred up a fine ash that the landscape, which had been flayed grey, absorbed as its due. I thought about the horrible picture of eternity that was given to us at school. It would last, so we were taught, the length of time it would take to wear down a mountain if the wing of a bird brushed against it once every hundred years. They have no idea how terrifying that is to children, who fear more than anything being unable to move. In the mineral flow that carried me off this morning, there was worse. The mere thought of a bird was impossible and the infinite expanse of stones was feeding on dust and becoming a mountain. Eternity was getting longer.

After a sharp pull of the wheel at the foot of a cliff, suddenly there was the valley. A great lake of thick grass where nothing was lacking from what would create our happiness on the morrow of the mists of time: rolls of wild honey on the high branches of the eucalyptus; ridged paths where white-robed children run; herds of cows sniffing the teff and the ponds; a few goats walking in step with a few masters, who lean on golden walking sticks; huts clinging to the low ribs of escarpments; branches that would produce smoke to caress lithe-bodied women; bouquets of shrubs; patches of coolness on the horizon that dance well back but refuse to recede. I describe the scene as François would have described a painted composition, in strata, we are perverted by our way of looking at pictures, which are odourless.

But it happened that I asked Salomon to stop, that he went off for a cigarette, and that I acquired fraudulently that hint of the earthly paradise. It is surely indescribable.

And so, tonight, I am content, though it's all stupid. I know that the huts are made of cow dung, the cattle are diseased, the goats feverish, the children starving, the women, servants and the men, porters. That they are able to eat not by putting their herds out to graze and by growing teff, but by lugging to the villages in the high plateaus the stones from which the tyrant's henchmen build their houses and businesses, hotels like this one where the pipes leak, the pool is cracked, and the flowers in the dining room are plastic. Beer is served there, and fake coffee ceremonies to the few Greek tourists who come to experience the Coptic Easter at Lalibela. Salomon, who knows people everywhere, says that many priests are considered to be thieves; they are entrusted with treasures, some of which God himself gave to their ministry a dozen centuries ago, nowadays their ornate gold stirs the greed of an unscrupulous government. The crosses and crowns are gradually disappearing from temples policed by men with Kalashnikovs, but evidently they can be bought; it's impossible to be armed and honest in Ethiopia, I quickly became aware of that in Addis.

Nevertheless I fall asleep slowly, the window open on the stridency of a handful of crickets, coiled in the idea of beauty. I touched it today and now it's as if it is not in my eyes but at my fingertips. One touches love, I can do it, in the same way.

Tomorrow, I get back on the long road to Addis Ababa. What's left for me to look at? It's time to make myself useful.

The ambassador closes the notebook, torn between finding this Marie interesting, in writing at least, and deploring the way that she's steeped in those remnants of a Christian education that nowadays sends so many young people to remote countries in search of impossible revelations. Nothing is less certain than the appearance of the first hominids in the Lalibela Valley, though one must acknowledge that the contrast between the scree that holds up the plateau and the greenness of the valley combines all the elements of a setting for Adam and Eve and later on, for Cain and Abel, especially since fratricidal wars have regularly marked the region. As for her love affair with the man called François, it seems to have been just, if not beautiful, which makes her death a form of privilege. Would she have gone on to betray him? An Abel could have taken the edge off her, Marie being still fresh and rather seductive. He sees her suddenly, precise down to the first wrinkles clawing at eyes at once so brown and so bright. A woman in red. An impromptu.

He pulls himself together, realizes she didn't write a word about her stay in Addis, or about meeting him in the salons

of the American embassy. She though had seemed worthy of
memory. Perhaps, in spite of his interesting postings and his
fairly erudite knowledge of the terrain, he has become someone bland, covered like the stones up there with an ash of
words, the diplomatic tone having finally dulled his wit.

Thus passes his desire to stay in the residence. To listen
to the fountain and to think in his turn about the colours
of the origin of the world. Ethiopia is no longer Abyssinia,
there's a famine to be dealt with, and in a while he will have
to inquire about where to send this notebook that belongs to
her estate. The question really answers itself, it's obvious that
he must send it to rue des Bouleaux in Laval, and that young
Pierre will have to endure the disagreeable reading of it. The
Canadian ambassador to Ethiopia, Sudan and Somalia will
also suppress the urge to start looking for a Burtukan in the
area around Lalibela. The evocation of that child, a type so
common in Ethiopia, was nothing but the epigraph of a
schoolmistress — a profession that is not safe from
mawkishness.

NINE

BUILT AT THE HEIGHT of the Canadian government's inferiority complex, the Lester B. Pearson building unfurls its shades of grey and its batrachian gaze down onto the Ottawa River and across to the Quebec shore, with a close-up of the federal parks and a long shot of the anthracite suburbs, a pleasant place to live within biking distance of the Gatineau Valley. On this autumn morning the eye can still rest on the rust and blonde and probably warm moss of this neutral zone, though it's hard to judge the weather from inside an air-conditioned office. Perched up there, Marcia Nelson, who still lives with her parents, experiences the first doubts inherent in her first job after graduation, here in the Department of Foreign Affairs. Yet she felt destined for this life, so well nourished was she at the University of Ottawa on the understated nostalgia for that same Pearson, who seems to have been at once a good man and a visionary, the way officers in the Canadian foreign service are required to be, or to become. In charge of diplomatic travel documents while she waits for her first posting abroad, she is musing over a dispatch from Addis Ababa, where the Canadian ambassador, who ought to be offering judicious advice that can be forwarded to the United Nations on ways to relieve the famine or bring about a truce in Eritrea, is getting worked up over the repatriation of the body of a road accident victim. For two days now Marcia, though highly bilingual, has been trying in vain to find any trace of a family for this woman named Marie, whom CARE seems to have recruited from another planet. Her file contains nothing but an address in Laval, to which phone calls go unanswered. At this very moment police are carrying on investigations in the vicinity, but the ambassador is getting impatient. The morgue in Addis is not a model of its kind, there are no daily flights via Europe, and before deciding on the route he has to know where the dead woman is supposed to end up.

Marcia upbraids herself for treating like a parcel the first dead person of her young career. The task should inspire her, but instead it's upsetting. The sun ought to go into hiding instead of being so softly beautiful over the valley of the Gatineau. Unlike her parents, Marcia is of the generation that sometimes dares to take the air of Quebec, amazed that it's breathable. But now it's giving off the smell of viscera. In this department people are prepared for death in foreign countries, it goes without saying because the planet is disturbed everywhere, but the decay that she's about to confront is of another order. It is that of a kind of unknown rival who was able to make her life a tragedy such as she, Marcia, will never experience. That's obvious when you go home to Nepean every night, and when Dad and Mom, civil servants too, are so lovable or loved, always.

When she comes back from lunch in the cafeteria, where everyone was scandalized over the assignment of a prestigious European embassy to an over-the-hill politician, the information finally arrives. This Marie was originally from Abitibi but has been an orphan for some years, she was briefly married but long since divorced, with no trace remaining of an individual named Tateossian, an immigrant who left on his own, the way he had arrived. She has only some very distant relatives, no doubt indifferent to her life or death, somewhere in Massachusetts. The Laval apartment, which she owns, is inhabited by an unemployed youth whom she seems to have supported for obscure reasons, they're unknown in any case to the concierge who supplied the few pieces of information that were later confirmed by the Office of the Registrar General. The police were unable to interview anyone else, the boy was away, the corridors deserted, the whole place is a desert.

Marcia advises the ambassador where the parcel is to be sent and by what route: Ethiopian Airlines to Frankfurt, then Air Canada to Montreal. While all that is being done they'll locate a morgue in Laval to receive the body and a funeral parlour to see to the formalities for the unclaimed dead, a problem to which such an operation surely holds all the keys.

The vague migraine that was threatening Marcia dissipates; someone places on her desk the always excessive bundle of her superior's African travels, which she must process with her eyes closed to the images of the starving villages to which he drags around his big belly and his outmoded opinions, feasting his eyes on the barely pubescent girls. What he doesn't dare to claim as an expense is their services, which he will in fact avoid paying for. He has sometimes had to hurry home because of gonorrhea, it's well known.

Around four p.m. the phone rings and a husky voice, barely that of a man, asks: "Are you Marcia Nelson?"

His name is Pierre. He explains with difficulty that he is the boy in Laval and that he wants to know if it's true that Marie died over there, as stated in a message the police had left with the concierge. There's been a mistake, he thinks, Marie is working in Addis Ababa, she never said anything to him about travelling outside that city. How could she have ended up in a Jeep hurtling into a canyon?

Marcia wonders who could have transferred this call to her, she's responsible for travel documents, not for special services of all kinds. It's some male who has taken off this

Friday afternoon and the receptionist is directing everyday matters to officers who can be relied on to do the job. Anyway, it's true that she is in a position to confirm whatever information the government of Canada possesses about this death.

She doesn't want to hang up first, the boy's state of mind worries her: he refuses to believe her and demands to see the body as soon as it arrives. But as what? While she tries in vain to extract a shred of identity — is he a son, a nephew? — she sees smoke, even flames rise up at the end of the Alexandria Bridge. Another of those matchstick houses in old Hull is burning, late in the season; generally it's midsummer storms that clear the region little by little of its shabby past. Now the strange voice becomes scorching too, as if it had caused the fire. Marcia leaves behind, against the rules, a little of her skin. She promises to call him back, she has to review the situation, she becomes insistent and motherly though she's barely twenty-five and has had no experience of solicitude until now.

There is a stain turning red above old Hull. A cremation must be violent. The body arrives on Sunday at midday, Marcia Nelson volunteers to take receipt of it at customs, it's not her responsibility but it suits her superior who is short of officers on the eve of the long Labour Day weekend. He takes note of her zeal, thinks she must be hoping for a promotion and it would be a good thing, she's the kind who sooner or later would take offence at the number of his trips to Africa, which everyone however has to admit are indispensable to maintaining Canada's impeccable reputation in humanitarian matters.

Because she wants to prowl around rue des Bouleaux, Marcia Nelson leaves Nepean on Sunday at dawn and instinctively turns onto the Quebec shore of the Ottawa

River. Gatineau, Montebello, Papineauville are asleep in their history-book gravity, villages crammed with the names of the most renowned of the French-Canadian bourgeoisie. Their illusions have so successfully postponed their country's death throes, for the time it takes to abdicate responsibility, that now they're considered to have possessed superior wisdom, whereas they were merely indecisive and tormented — like Pearson himself, from whose myth Marcia is reluctantly breaking free. She, who has inherited all his dreams, who is young and masters both languages, eager to serve the public good, having read and absorbed Anne Hébert and Margaret Atwood, certain from the outset that the two peoples can be reconciled, is nonetheless experiencing this journey along the other shore as vaguely menacing. The menace becomes clearer in the long series of blighted villages leading to Laval — villages that are awake. Suddenly, Marcia is driving her Honda clumsily and is now constantly being passed by vans, she asks so timidly in French for a muffin and coffee that a good girl will naturally serve her in English at the Dunkin' Donuts in a mall whose parking lot is already full, at ten a.m. on Sunday. It takes her a while to find rue des Bouleaux, in a neighbourhood under development that no one's familiar with, not even at the service stations.

She parks near a bed of begonias where there's not a soul in sight, and sits in the car for long minutes, stunned by the pink brick apartment blocks, all identical, all silent, all decked out with a circumflex hat above their wide and ostentatious doors, all no doubt signed up with the same chemical maintenance service for the lawns, whose green is withering uniformly; no autumn leaf will linger there because the trees, if there are any, are planted at the back of these bunkers that are the colour of poor-quality

Renaissance prints. Marcia is stunned because rue des Bouleaux is a precise replica of Pine or Birch or Oak Street in the neighbourhood that was grafted onto Nepean's side five years ago and was soon filled with a new generation of civil servants, most of them from the other provinces. As if the plans not only for the houses but also for the places themselves came from one catalogue, inspired by settlement camps in the occupied territories, which smother their anxiety by means of tidy lines: camps for refugees from the quiet middle class.

She doesn't dare to stroll through this entrenchment where all the windows are covered with the same blinds. Here people can observe you through half-closed slats without one eyelash moving in the building. A cold volley of shots that she, who has no reason to be on rue des Bouleaux, should shy away from, her department hasn't asked her to investigate, only take care of the formalities at Mirabel. But Marcia Nelson feels that her life of adventure is finally beginning, her life as an external affairs officer prepared to go further than required by duty. She enters 10,005 and rings the concierge's bell to the right of the front door, laughter bursts out, inappropriate here in such a gloomy place, and a faint aroma of peppers fried in oil. It makes her hungry, which is also inappropriate. It's obvious that she's going to disturb this woman at the beginning or in the middle of the Sunday meal. Her name suggests that she's Catholic, so interrupting her is something that should not be done without some powerful reason, which is nonexistent here. For Marcia though, the moment is intoxicating, unique, she must seize it because it's unlikely to come back — on Canadian soil anyway — and she prepares to find the words to apologize, to invent an emergency.

Fatima greets her however as if she'd been expecting her.

It's aperitif time and she's drinking it in the company of a man her age, forty or so, whose deep-set, laughing eyes contrast with his stringy complexion, the type whose looks are described as "Mediterranean." Marcia's arrival is well timed, she and Felipe have been talking about the events, word of which has spread to the upper floors, a visit by the police attracts attention in a peaceful spot like this.

Fatima is voluble, abetted perhaps by alcohol. What is this business they want to involve her in? She's been asked to identify the body because she, the concierge, is apparently the only source of credible information. She'll do it because she's obliged to, she has no choice, but she's getting fed up with 10,005 rue des Bouleaux, which has the evil eye. In fact she'll be leaving next month, with Felipe, who owns a bar and bistro near the Plateau Mont-Royal, she'll move in upstairs with him. That will be fine. She'll be a waitress, wash dishes if necessary. She knows something about that kind of business, her father ran a drinking place in Vienna where he had finally settled down after a series of immigrations. If she thinks about it carefully, the clientele of the forlorn who went there, some of them so deprived of women that they had their eyes on her as a child, were much better people than the underhanded gang who live in this building, all of them turned in on their own probably sordid secrets. And stingy on top of it.

"I'll just send the kid back to the States and I'm out of here." Marcia learns of the existence of Virginia, takes pity on her loneliness in this place where only adults live. She has found an easy way to make Fatima gossip more informatively about the inhabitants of the building and in particular about Pierre, whose influence on the child has the concierge worried. She'd known boys like him in the past, who pretended to take her out walking and ended up asking her to touch them. Pierre gave Virginia a little quartz watch, a cheap trinket that excites the little girl. Now she waits for him every evening. He doesn't always come home, he hangs out in the arcades with queers, maybe he's a hustler himself. Felipe saw him once leaning against a car near the vacant lot over there, he was with a fat guy covered with tattoos, the kind who likes being beaten with chains, apparently blood turns them on. What would he do to her, to the little girl? You never know.

Fatima talks more discreetly about the woman on the fourth floor, who used to be in politics and has decorated her apartment so nicely. Pierre did the painting, but she finally kicked him out. He didn't seem to work very hard, you'd often spot his lanky silhouette on the balcony in the sun. She'd seen so many like him in her father's café, men who were soft except for their pricks, who fantasized about their talent for seducing older women. But that distinguished woman wasn't taken in, she fired him and a good thing too. As for the dead woman, what Fatima thinks is that he tried the same thing with her but she took off instead of kicking him out, nobody knows why.

Or maybe he's her son, though the concierge doesn't think so. She saw them side by side in a corner store at the beginning of summer, his hand was on her hip, as if she was his girlfriend. With those low-cut red dresses she wore maybe she brought problems on herself.

In any event, Fatima mutters more softly, as if to herself, he drives the people around him crazy, trouble piles up, it's unbearable. One of the owners tried to murder his wife with fire, the way those barbarians in India do. And there's been a lot of petty thievery, which isn't normal, only a few delivery-men come to 10,005, the concierge keeps a close eye on them, the robberies must have been an inside job. The owners' meetings are becoming stormy, people are starting to criticize Fatima. So before they drive her away, before the boy rapes the little girl, she's leaving, with her friend Felipe. She certainly wouldn't want to be around if he caused another death. It's the fault of that Pierre, finally, if the woman died from moving away from him and into a dangerous country.

Marcia's not sure she has understood everything, she was brought up in a climate devoid of superstition, she can't imagine having a conversation about the evil eye. Anyway, it's only good manners to leave Fatima and Felipe to their meal.

Far from being haunted, the corridor is ripe with the scent of peonies mixed with disinfectant, one of the new concoctions the maintenance company employees like, you can see why. Marcia doesn't experience the thrill she was hoping for from her incursion into such foreign territory. The air is perfectly conditioned, a big mirror by the elevator sends back the image of a twentyish Anglo in a flowered skirt drifting above flat heels, a beige blouse over a slender bosom, straight shoulder-length hair, a permanent, faintly pink smile. She thinks she looks ordinary, whereas salesladies find her definitely pretty, she looks good in whatever she tries on, it gives them a rest from all the inelegance they see parade by. In her own opinion though she looks more like someone visiting a hospital.

Marcia decides to check out the building the way the heroine of an action movie would do, to make something happen. She'll go to Marie's in fact just to fix in her mind's eye the image of a threshold the dead woman would have crossed. Suddenly she realizes that she's never seen a corpse. Families no longer expose their dead, urns are replacing coffins more and more, from their finest photos the departed bid farewell with beautiful smiles and in excellent health. It's morbid and unseemly to be curious about the condition of a body, waxy and disfigured, but she can't help herself.

Two or three times she paces the fourth floor, nothing is moving there. It's a garret like any other, more antiseptic than the hallway in a convent, where the air always carries some trace of the sweat that flows abundantly in individuals who are overly chaste. She takes the elevator down, disappointed but relieved to be back in the sunlight. She opens the door of the Honda, briefly lets out the torrid air that was scorching the leatherette, observes 10,005 rue des Bouleaux for the last time. Suddenly Pierre looms up, as if he had passed through the wall stage left. It's him, thin, musky, poured into bleached jeans, with a swelling at the crotch from an erection or a knife. As if they were on a date he gives her a little bow. A handsome specimen, desirable but, alas, the type that's never interested in her. She escapes.

So ends her adventure. At Mirabel, the customs officials don't even ask her to accompany the box to the morgue, because the police are taking care of the follow-up and the identification. She won't see Marie. Once repatriated, a dead person is no longer under Foreign Affairs jurisdiction. Marcia drives home along the Ontario side of the Ottawa River, a view for her mind's eye only, because the waterway is invisible from the highway.

For your world to be exciting, your name has to be Fatima.

TEN

THE ORGANIZERS of the benefit for AIDS research had hesitated for a long time before deciding on a maison de la culture in Laval. In spite of the good-sized lobby, the well-equipped stage, the efficient ticket office, it seemed shrunken because the auditorium could seat only a hundred and fifty. The idea of holding this first public rally around the tragedy of a disease that was about to become epidemic had come to them in July, from images of Live Aid, the rock concert broadcast worldwide that had placed the Ethiopian famine, until then tolerated, at the forefront of reasons for global indignation. The flow of emergency funds, sustained by millions of guilty viewers, had multiplied a hundredfold.

In the kitchen of the Montreal clinic where the plan had first taken shape, there had been just one volunteer at first, a fat little woman nobody listened to though they left it to her to assist the dying; she had pointed out that there was no equivalence between the pictures of Ethiopian babies dying at the breasts of their emaciated mothers — sublime modern version of the massacre of the innocents — and the rare photos of those dying of AIDS, with their sores suppurating from an excess of accursed sperm, a disturbing modern version of the punishment of Sodom. They told her that Montreal, along with San Francisco, was one of the rare sites of gay liberation in North America and that women's ability to empathize with homosexuals was higher there, for reasons having to do with the kind of matriarchy long since in effect among old-stock Quebeckers. A good many mothers preferred to imagine their sons quickly coupling and uncoupling at the baths rather than clinging for long nights to the curves of another woman and worse, combining love with ejaculation. It was possible and even probable that they could count on these middle-aged women — who formed public opinion by monopolizing the radio phone-in shows — to create a climate of forgiveness, another Québécois specialty, in this case stemming from the ancestral masochism of a colonized people. And the climate of forgiveness was the necessary ingredient, the key to a reversal of the situation, that is access to the public funds controlled by those gentlemen whose own sexual orientation was, in appearance at least, the furthest thing from deviant.

Having put the fat little woman in her place, a young doctor sure of his psychosociological facts had approached television stations about broadcasting the show, but he'd had to choke back his arrogance almost at the outset. The biggest public station, the federal one, had turned him down politely with references to administrative policies that had no room for medical research among the good works it agreed to support. The danger of creating a precedent was too great, they'd be overwhelmed with requests from associations that support victims of breast cancer or heart disease or childhood disorders far more unbearable than this AIDS business which, after all, affects only a minute segment of their audience. As for the biggest private station, the one that seemed to print so easily millions of dollars for various telethons, its brass had sent a very dynamic and understanding spokesperson who had assured him of the warmest welcome at a future appointment if in the meantime he could come up with a few solid sponsors. He was well aware without having to consult the fat little woman that he wouldn't even get through the door of the PR department of a financial institution or even a pharmaceutical company. They'd be happy enough to take the money for research, but would refuse to display any sympathy for the plague victims, as their science ought to go instead to making them disappear.

He'd had to fall back on the limited circles of friends. The only openly gay member of the legislature and two or three of his more discreet but obliging colleagues had been able eventually to reach an agreement with Radio-Québec, whose educational mandate had always been interpreted flexibly. The program managers, while reacting favourably to the plan after a week of resistance inside the institution, had however insisted on a delayed broadcast, ostensibly because the fall schedule was full, but in fact so they could maintain the possibility of censorship. The performers who had agreed to appear for the benefit of AIDS research were minor stars, and the risk of going live, even with scripts approved in advance, was too high. Families would be watching.

And so they had to resign themselves to Radio-Québec, which was after all better than nothing. Next came the rounds of the big auditoriums whose vast size was a handicap in such a situation. Without the excitement created by a major broadcaster, and with just a handful of so-so performers, they couldn't expect to sell thousands of tickets. The doctor came back sheepishly to the clinic kitchen and the fat little woman, who was as modest as she was magnanimous, suggested they choose one of the maisons de la culture. They're popular with the penniless and have the right values, and they'd provide a positive audience that would get the struggle off to a good start. Of course the admission would barely cover expenses, practically nothing would be left for research, but would it be better to cancel?

Silence around the table, where the fat little woman had set down a bowl of the season's magnificent black cherries, none of the six dared to touch: to touch something that was round, red, garnet, flesh — breasts, nipples, lips to be swallowed mindlessly, lying down with another, for an hour or for life. From now on that would be their ordeal. Between them and the taste of things was a constantly thickening skin, a viscous cataract that kept them from gazing deeply into the eyes of their patients, patients who were submissive, resigned, humiliated by their sores.

As if she were attached to that silent wire, a nurse began a monologue. "Still, a lot of them defy the people around them." There was one who during his lifetime had organized a farewell ceremony to which he'd invited all the relatives and friends he could think of, greeting them from a wheelchair as they paraded in, his withered limbs nearly naked under a loincloth. Only two teenage girls, braving their families' terrified looks, had dared to kiss him. He'd stood up for a minute, leaning against the buffet where the gathering comforted themselves with cold cuts and wine, and announced that he was leaving them for Hell. His voice was reedy, no one had protested. They believed him. Another had orchestrated an impressive funeral for himself in an Outremont church attended by Quebec's rich and powerful. A number of them seemed to be fixated on giving in to death while spitting in the faces of others.

Rather than put on a show, the literary type among them had ventured to say, what they should do is write an old-fashioned mystery play that would deal with present-day passions.

The curtain would go up. A child would open a large illustrated book in a red cover with gold lettering, like the sacred histories of our youth, and try to study the lives that end well and those that end badly. The grace of a clean, white death, barely morphined so there could be one last smile, would be depicted there as one that is usually reserved for those who have lived lives of renunciation. It would evoke the lives of young parents with one or two children, who drove used sedans, cooked green vegetables, worked their fingers to the bone to pay for daycare, took in the free concerts at the jazz festival, gave to Centraide, committed adultery occasionally and responsibly, their consciences not at rest but without excess; it would be a celebration of the just of our time, when saintliness is no longer what it used to be. But — and this would be the magnificent lesson presented by the tableau — the disgrace of a disgusting, contaminated death, of truncated bodies from which the soul is driven long before the end, would not be reserved for the wicked. On the right-hand page, between the illuminations, the child would read aloud the musical bubbles, the comic book of existences scattered and light as pistils, that settle on their neighbour and touch him and touch him again, sometimes to the point of fiery black orgasm, the kind that brings death amid pus and horror. And that, as an androgynous choir would tell the assembled crowd, was the life of other just men of the present day. As they hadn't known pleasure, those who chose a white death take their leave surrounded by regret, while those condemned to a sullied death experience none of it.

The child would proceed from page to page without choosing, the choir would recite a metallic Kyrie, then he would turn to the crowd and ask them to list their fears. In the hall the long-haired, the cool, the open-minded, the sexually liberated could boo, mock, walk out, convinced that they belong to the circle of the brave, that they've finished with celestial punishments and drivel about the apocalypse. But most wouldn't dare to make love that night and maybe in nights to come. Not all orgasms are worth dying from.

Obviously that was unacceptable, the notion of a grand tragic script and a stripped-down production. The cause that the clinic wanted to serve threatened to end the festival of a generation and of its laid-back progeny, instead they should lighten the atmosphere. Suggest lots of songs, both harmonious and angry, on the model of Live Aid, invite a few poets who can always be counted on to break down cynicism, and banish speeches except for one by a great actor who had agreed to serve as spokesperson and who would read, at the end, a few stanzas by an unknown.

Around the table people breathed more easily. Hands reached out to the bowl of black cherries. Someone mentioned a sensitization device that was spreading across the United States. During demonstrations of solidarity, a big quilt was spread out, each section bearing the name of someone who had died of AIDS — often a pseudonym, because a number of families didn't want the publicity. The effect was gripping but reassuring too, the quilt being a symbol of the prodigal child's return to the lap of the grandmother who rocks her memories of the child and frees him from the shadows. Who but the Americans could invent something so ridiculous, said a French trainee who had read Lacan and who refused outright to mask the depths of human despair. They could do better, and he suggested as a background anonymous photos of some of the dead. Others would be able to identify them or not, but at least they'd be looking death in the face. Which was accepted.

So it was that Simon, the out politician, agreed to the scenario and suggested putting Gabrielle Perron on the committee of honour for the evening. Having left politics after fine service in the Ministry of Cultural Affairs, her name could now be one of those that give nonprofit organizations credibility because their connections are wide-ranging and they can't be suspected of serving personal ambition. What's more, she was a woman and her sex was underrepresented in the circles concerned about the advance of AIDS, which was wreaking havoc among males.

Among her former colleagues, Simon was one of the few Gabrielle wanted to see again. Homosexuals freed from clandestinity are, at least in adulthood, rather exquisite creatures. Simon had a talent for the frivolous, he could read, understand and interpret all the constitutional theses but avoid the tiresome people who draw them up, a distance those same tiresome people were glad to respect in return, so insecure was their own sexuality and so fearful were they of debates with an unpredictable speaker whose superior civility would emphasize their stuffy awkwardness. Simon also had a genius for friendship, he bestowed it far and wide and had some left over for absorbing confidences, from both the suffering and the superficial. You had only to embrace him and already you'd feel relieved of some turmoil or doubt, for in his company, lightness was a duty. Yet neither Gabrielle nor the rest of her delegation had ever solved the mystery surrounding his companion, an American who raised Arabian horses near Trois-Rivières, who didn't appear in public and of whom Simon revealed nothing, not even during the most alcoholic tête-à-têtes with his closest women friends. Some said he was crippled and violent, but that was simply ignorant speculation to comfort those who were jealous of so much beauty. Because Simon was also the handsomest boy in the National Assembly, tall, slim, radiant and dark, the kind that sensual women like. "You're a loss to humanity," Gabrielle often joked, though she appreciated the absence of desire between them. They spoke frankly to one another. In fact Simon had often told her that he disagreed with her leaving politics, something he couldn't — or wouldn't — understand.

They'd got together then, for old times' sake, at the

Continental where Gabrielle Perron's return to Quebec City, even for just a few hours, had turned a few heads and started some rumours. Over glasses of Brouilly, how could she resist the straightforward but provocative request by her favourite? She got busy as in the good old days, drawing up a list of people to approach, suggesting the course of events, estimating sources of funds or exchanges of services. She also played sociologist. The disease, she said, was emerging just as homosexuals seemed to be settling down, starting to demand the right to marriage and even to have children, dreaming of normality. It would be interesting to see how this new behaviour would be reconciled with the sordid life on the fringes to which AIDS was consigning them. The political calculations by the various groups may have explained why it was hard to plan their evening, when powerful images were liable to confirm the confusion between homosexuality and depravity. Still, she missed the motivating forces that could be sensed in depravity. "How do you feel now, as a member of the gay community? As if you were living in the cocoon of a religious order, following a rule and performing your rituals to tunes by the Singing Nun?" Simon said she was more or less right, but in his opinion an obsession with community was the price to pay for making the system bend. He reminded her of the assembly debates on including sexual orientation among the grounds for nondiscrimination to be inscribed in the charter of human rights. She sighed again at the depressing prospect of chipping away that was always imposed by any search for the common good. She'd been right to move away from it.

"Anyway," said Simon, "let me reassure you. I don't want to get married or adopt a little orphan. Now less than ever."

He'd stated it as a joke but by the end of the bottle of Brouilly, Gabrielle knew there was no mistake. She had just been given the most moving confidence possible by Simon, whose laughing mouth had grimaced slightly. Things must have been going badly in Trois-Rivières. But asking would have endangered their friendship. She merely repeated that Simon could use her name and her former title, that she'd help organize the evening if he wanted. A speech was out of the question though, no matter how brief.

She took a walk in Old Quebec, to sober up before getting back in her car. The blast of tourists still masked the charm of the place; she saw one spit onto the wheel of a calèche and heard another making fatuous remarks in front of some wonders of Inuit art on exhibition at the Brousseaus, who were impervious to the commercial trivialization of the genre. She'd be better off going into Simons and poking around in the new fall accessories, the hats whose secrets are known to the store's buyers, the gloves that in the interior light of Quebec City give you the hands of Laure Clouet. She bought gloves and hat in rusty brown, though she knew that back in Laval, she'd never wear them.

Without really admitting it to herself, Gabrielle was going to enjoy being involved in a good deed. Particularly because AIDS was now a little like what sovereignty had been in the days of the pioneers. The cause would make it possible to separate the fearful from the brave. Her old acquaintances, those who had given up on changing the world and were now tending to their gardens or their investments, declared their sympathy — their hearts and their reading were still in the right place — but claimed to be terribly busy. The children were entering their teens and going through identity crises, the start of the university year was a gridlock of meetings, their old parents were sick and dependent, they themselves worked hard on behalf of theatres or orchestras that, despite their reputation, were

experiencing severe financial problems — something a former culture minister in a government that had initiated the
era of cutbacks ought to know. A brilliant way to make her
step back, to force her to appeal to those generous souls
who, dreaming of a sunny Quebec, could not be insensitive
to these young men who were living on borrowed time and
cruelly deprived of the chance of living until the great day.
They gave sums, small and sometimes large, promised to be
present. They confirmed the existence of decency, that greatest of mysteries.

Strong arms were needed for building the sets and
Gabrielle had the idea of dispatching Pierre. At the end of
the summer she had closed her door to him; there'd been no
scandal, it was like turning a page, and she'd talked with him
only briefly when they met in the lobby, about Marie's
departure and her death. A stupid accident. What would
become of him? He wasn't related to the woman, the estate
would kick him out of the apartment once some official had
determined where her belongings would go, to the State or
some distant relations. He'd go back up north, he said.
Gabrielle didn't believe it, he was now part of the city's
fringe, but she wouldn't question him further. In fact she
hoped to see him disappear; he'd been a vulgar passing sexual fancy for which she now reproached herself. He had a
way of looking at her now that placed her among those old
ladies who haven't lost their looks. She regained the advantage by treating him as a handyman and a pal, as well as
teaching him a couple of things about preventing a disease
that could threaten him some day, in his roaming.

Pierre turned out to be an excellent assistant to the video
editor, a volunteer from Radio-Canada, carrier of the virus
and released from his everyday activities by colleagues

openly compassionate but secretly terrified of his mere presence. Some disinfected any equipment he had used, producers gave their instructions by telephone, most of the time he ate alone. In contrast, Pierre as a pupil was attentive and intense, overcharged with interest because of some hunger for danger. The plan was to slowly bring up on a large upstage screen the features, confused at first, then clear and sharp, of some AIDS victims of the past two years. Some were known, others weren't. The editor had run into some of them at the clinic, the only one where the doctors told the whole truth.

Denis, a grizzled thirtysomething with dusty blue eyes behind thick glasses, his neck venous and seemingly twisted, had been one of the first to die. He was a painter, he inscribed on his canvas, in shades of grey and flesh, the walls that he came up against in life. A silent soul under sentence of death.

Marc, bald, dry, his gaze like knots on a parched vine, ended up blackened as if from third-degree burns. He was a journalist, of average talent but highly cultivated, assigned to rewrite reporters with bylines who ignored him.

Michel, with the kindly mug of a busker, a child who never tired of teaching other children at the university. He was a biologist and didn't forgive his science for missing out on his disease. He was furious, for once, when he died.

Yves, his face half-hidden by his long, tragic, manicured hands, in the hazy pose of the dying, already snatched up by the ether. He was a writer, read less and less, for him the virus had been a suicide of rare elegance.

And François, of whom there were no close-up photos but who was very recognizable, with his stooped height, sharp profile softened by flyaway hair, talking to an invisible audience. He was the best-known art critic in Quebec, prone to having sex with his disciples, most of whom were now infected but still under his spell.

"I know him," said Pierre. The editor laughed. How could he? The world of François Dubeau had nothing to do with that of a dropout from up north now a resident of Laval, a suburb rather impervious to intellectuals unless they'd settled there early and raised small families on their small salaries. François was anything but that.

Bristling, Pierre asked a lot of questions about the man. He had recognized him beyond any doubt, he'd been Marie's lover, the tall cheerful guy who marked off the garden's seasons with her in the little house where Pierre's mother had dumped him, the man who talked with her about Abyssinia and whose presence he'd eventually grown accustomed to, though they never really got used to each other.

It was just a double life, the editor would have said had he believed it. Suddenly Pierre understood its refined seams, the nights spent this way or that, the spaces reserved for one and for the others, the sentences slipped on like clothing, according to the climate, according to the clients. Having sperm in common, all the same. Marie had no doubt consented to the game, she never seemed bothered by her lover's absences, she made no plans. Her lie added to his made a mountain of waste between yesterday's child and his memories. For the adult he was now becoming, reminiscences in the form of excreta.

The smell of sweat was in fact filling the little office that adjoined the auditorium. Two members of the organizing committee had just come in, engaged in a virulent debate on how to use the small profits expected from the show. The editor went on impassively lining up photos and dreaming of the effect he wanted to create, similar to that of Thierry Kuntzel's fantastic video on the death of the Swiss writer Robert Walser, a piece that had given new life to the art of the dissolve.

ELEVEN

THE POLITICAL EVENT of the autumn made its first appearance in the arts sections of some English-language newspapers and magazines. A young anglophone Montrealer — that rare creature of direct British descent — brought out a magnificent book on the Canadian psyche, entitled *French Bastard*. Stunningly intelligent and subjective, it defied the conciliatory syrup that had been flowing from the leading anglophone nonfiction writers ever since the 1945 publication of *Two Solitudes*. In it, Susan Finney made mincemeat of the theory underlying MacLennan's novel and even more, those of his followers. In their opinion it was the distance between social classes that had poisoned any attempt at a loving fusion between the respective offspring of Canada's two founding peoples and consequently, kept the political divide between conquerors and conquered from being filled; whence the idea, highly conventional but even after half a century not yet hackneyed, that the enrichment of francophones and their progress towards some kind of economic equality would lead to growing interpenetration between descendants of these offspring. Which sooner or later would snuff out the collective desire for separation.

Aside from a few details, such as the still mostly anglophone ownership of houses on Summit Circle or country mansions on Brome Lake, the new writer reminded her readers, we had however achieved financial equality. Any interpenetration was still limited though, and generally ended in the most poisonous divorces, as any specialist in family law, with whom Susan Finney had spent a lot of time, could testify. In her opinion, the lasting error of the political scientists was to sublimate their own anemic sexual appetites while they wallowed in subsidized Canadian conferences, which had kept them from coming to grips with the notion of desire. Its absence, so striking in heterosexual relationships between francophones and anglophones, had thus escaped them. Aside from some passing superficial oddities, analogous to vacation flings, interpenetration hadn't happened. If one compared the customs of linguistically mixed and linguistically homogeneous suburban couples, one would note that the English-French connection was the one that would fade most rapidly and most surely. And blandness, she declared, the smell of poorly aired closets that's given off by genitals at rest, was well on its way to becoming the existential definition of Canada.

She for her part saw no problem, therefore offered no solutions. She simply set out a masterful description of the peculiar blockage of the fibres or nerve endings in the pelvic area. It had been noted by observers of brief news items that crimes of passion between francophones and anglophones were practically nonexistent, even when squabbles over money reached a paroxysm. Which also explained the damp squib that terrorism in Quebec had been, lacking any genuine will to destroy.

Susan Finney's book took a totally exceptional turn in the chapter devoted to her own attempt to verify degrees of intercultural desire. She told how she had forced herself to become a sovereigntist, by joining the party but mainly by offering herself as a transit between the "two solitudes," the MacLennan cliché being common currency in all political circles. She'd become an adviser and had set her heart on a cabinet minister who rumour had it was a big-time stud who'd fooled around with her in the back of a government plane one evening after a pointless trip to the Baie des

Chaleurs. He'd tried to seduce the old-stock anglophones and in the end had to be content with getting it off with Susan Finney. The description of their carryings-on attained pornographic exuberance, as free flowing and high performance as you could wish for during traditional interpenetration, but toned down while fooling around with sodomy. Even between two famished temperaments in still young bodies that were exploring one another for the first time, she had noted, desire could not transcend a threshold that was invisible but genuine, and abnormally low. Susan Finney had pursued the experiment to the point of conceiving a child, the French bastard of her title. The book would reveal the child's existence to its progenitor, whose anonymity she otherwise protected. "My child," she concluded, "is in radiant good health. But no one stops me in the street to tell me how gorgeous a baby it is. I push the carriage of a creature who is imperceptible, as if volatile. It is my future and yours. It won't kill us."

Gabrielle had a clear memory of Susan Finney, who was once connected with a ministry close to her own. She was amazed at what she read — a few magazine excerpts and ecstatic reviews. The impassioned style, the gritty way of hijacking the political debate, the exhibitionism that was the antithesis of Canadian tradition, should have been the acts of a beautiful sex kitten. But as the public could now observe on its screens, there was nothing of a Mata Hari about Susan Finney. She was more like an apple. Timid sea green eyes, plump cheeks, a cherub's colouring, dirty-blonde hair that fell straight onto a cotton blouse, full flowered skirts in summer, pleated ones in winter, sensible shoes at all times. The body seemed clumsy but, as men will confide, girls who are ordinary and chubby are often wilder and more unrestrained in bed than those who emulate scrawny fashion models.

Still, if she'd had to predict a literary career for Susan Finney back then, it would have been as a writer of cookbooks or gardening manuals. And here she was, invited on all the talk shows, facing psychoanalysts, psychosociologists, constitutionalists and journalistic analysts of all sorts, chattering exceptionally well in both languages, buttoning lips and shutting traps, and once her debating partner had been cornered, bringing him to a full stop with sexological references that were apparently irrefutable and foreign to them all.

In Quebec, which revelled in its tolerance of politicians' morals, where the press ignored gossip about their extramarital flings or even about their family happiness, a kind of erotic fever was suddenly running through even the news sections, with insinuations as to the identity of the minister, who was immediately recognized, or phrases referring to the thesis of *French Bastard*. Gabrielle wouldn't allow herself to buy the book but Madeleine, for once taking an interest in politics because it sounded like a sex scandal, had gone through it zealously. On the phone, she burbled with enthusiasm. She drew some strange lessons from the thesis about Canadian blandness.

"That Susan Finney's right, you know, and the sovereignists should have thought about it before. They have to show the world that reconciliation and the growing integration into Canada is going to create the most colourless people on earth. A nightmare, a new form of the revenge of the cradle!"

But Madeleine was wrong. As Susan Finney had noted, because of the absence of desire, Gabrielle explained patiently, there would be very few of those attractive and colourless children. Aside from the literary episode, she had no interest in this thesis, in fact she wondered if Finney's undeniable talent wasn't being secretly used by opposing forces still intent on destabilizing the party. The government's mandate would soon be up, the troops were worn out from the demands of power, the option was languishing in the polls and now the slight amount of intellectual energy still liable to be harnessed was being exhausted on a banal sex story that claimed to be a powerful symbolic discovery! But Madeleine stuck by her guns. "All I know is, you haven't kept up the healthy tradition of fornication in Nouvelle-France. Just when some real urges are being talked about . . ."

Which allowed the conversation to turn to Madeleine's own most recent urges and let harmony prevail, as usual, when they hung up.

With the blinds all open onto mid-September, the apartment was drinking in a greenish early evening, a foam of low sky. Gabrielle stepped onto the balcony but came right back in, shivering. She realized for the first time that summer would always be shorter here on rue des Bouleaux, looking down on the river. Then she recalled the chill that comes over small children, even during heat waves, when they're at the top of a Ferris wheel, swaying in midair. It took her back to that height, to the verge of a faint nausea. There was no place to get off and no one to start the wheel moving again.

In the library she switched on the lamps whose power she had studied so as to reproduce the warmth of winter lighting, especially on stormy nights with wuthering winds.

What books to plunge into? The grotesque debate that was upsetting her former associates, over a book in fact, managed to blight the magic of the place. Turning her into a nostalgic old woman, the kind she loathed. Her lost and better bygone days were there before her, on the shelves reserved for books on palingenesis, that magnificent scholarly word she had dared to get close to though she'd never studied Greek or, in the narrow schools she'd attended, elegant French. She found there, intact and as mellow as the memory of a perfume, the route that had allowed her, a bus driver's daughter, to propose for what Quebec would become an interpretation that had won her the unanimous congratulations of the French jury before whom she'd defended her thesis.

It had all started at the time of her first contact lenses and her long hair tied back in a big bow, at the end of her college days. A literature teacher, an intemperate Balzac enthusiast, was constantly boring his students with the notion that the crossroads of all modern science, no less, could be found in the preface to *La Comédie humaine*. The students didn't understand a word of this pretentious-sounding gobbledegook wherein Balzac declared that he was describing variations on the human species the way others described those of animals. The teacher had nonetheless ordered them to pick one of the scientific references the novelist had amassed, a veritable name-dropping for nineteenth century Paris salons, and write an essay on it. Chance had sent Gabrielle to one Charles Bonnet (1720–1793), a Swiss naturalist and philosopher whom Balzac considered to be a genius for having formulated a theory of the world as "an interlocking of similar components," where "animal vegetates as does plant." Which made of Bonnet a brilliant disciple of Leibniz, improving upon his thesis on continuity in the universe, a systematic mind perfectly suited to the great novelist seeking coherence for the thousands of characters in his boundless work.

Gabrielle, who didn't think she had a scientific mind, had taken an interest in Bonnet as she would have in a game. Aside from his birth and death dates, she found nothing on the man's life in Quebec's meagre libraries. She had been content to imagine him as dismal and destitute until years later, long after she'd defended her thesis, which did not contain these frivolous notions, in the public university library in Geneva, where she was able to consult the originals of his works and two amazing paintings. One was a portrait in oil signed by one Jens Juel, revealing Bonnet as a handsome man with a high forehead and an arrogant pout, obviously acquainted with the finest hair curlers, tailors and manicurists, the open book under his hand appearing less central to the composition than his emerald silk lapels and the frothing lace of his shirt at the wrist. The other, dated 1780 and signed by Simon Malgo, was a rather insipid and green "*Vue des environs du lac Léman du côté du Midi prise de la demeure de M. C. Bonnet à Genthod, à une lieue au Nord de Genève,*" whose very existence attested to the bourgeois comfort that philosophers, it's true, rarely spurn and often seek.

But in the days when she was obeying her literature professor, Gabrielle had available only a few titles and some resumés of the work of Charles Bonnet, whose treatise entitled *Palingénésie philosophique, ou idées sur l'état passé et sur l'état futur des êtres vivants*, published in Geneva in 1770, presented a cosmogonic doctrine uniting geology, embryology, eschatology, psychology and metaphysics to illustrate the continual rebirth of living beings, while at the same time considering in that endless repetition, their capacity for evolution. British dictionaries attribute to Bonnet the authorship of the term, while French dictionaries assign it rather — and quite shamelessly, given the truth of the dates — to the Lyon philosopher Pierre-Simon Ballanche, whose *Essais de palingénésie sociale*, published between 1827 and 1829, are today considered to be pale copies of Bonnet's thinking, distorted what's more by blasts of religious mysticism and the digressions of a dilettante more concerned with impressing his friend Madame de Récamier than with contributing to scientific progress. Balzac, though his contemporary, had been right to prefer his predecessor in palingenesis.

The dissertation was supposed to be limited to five pages, but Gabrielle was able to make such good use of the few scraps of knowledge on her subject that the Balzac scholar gave her an exceedingly high mark. And from then on, the fine word "palingenesis" was a secret asset, proof that she could perhaps become an intellectual — to her, the most amazing destiny but one which she didn't think she could dream of because, as a rule, she'd have had to descend from other intellectuals to get there or, failing that, to be a boy who'd come to the attention of teachers in a classical college reserved for boys. At the time, no woman in Quebec had published a serious work of nonfiction or taught at the graduate level in the departments that manufactured intellectuals.

She had become a sociologist anyway, agreeing to study social statistics, which at the time passed for the major doctrine in a discipline that claimed to be scientific. It was not until she arrived in France, during an early conversation with her thesis director, that, to impress him, she had dared to utter the word "palingenesis" to describe her reading of the cultural renaissance Quebec seemed to be experiencing. The master had been delighted and had continued to be during the following two years, helping her to put that old notion in contact with contemporary sociological thinking, at the same time encouraging her to restore the reputation of Ballanche, some of whose spiritual, if not religious, investigations could be found in Madaule and possibly in Poulantzas.

In short, she had landed her doctorate with rather disconcerting ease, given her background and the earlier limits to her aspirations. And she'd come home to the shores of the St. Lawrence, to her country whose turmoil she would contribute to that much more because she had now mastered a scientific explanation for a sovereignist movement whose inconsistencies and chaos the fearful curmudgeonly analysts who still reigned supreme at the reins of newspapers denounced.

The very French weight of her intellectual trappings had however quickly lightened. In the new university, professor and students were the same age and the liveliness of their discussions was no less striking than the lightness of their morals. The sexual revolution often moved faster than the revolt against Canadian shackles or capitalist exploitation, her years of teaching were less studious than her years of thesis writing had been. Palingenesis was gradually reduced to a vague memory before it became, in politics, a useless object. Because first and foremost it was necessary to speak in a way that people understood.

In a waiting room a few weeks earlier, she'd been leafing through one of those magazines that specialize in treating females as brainless, which offered a long list of therapies for sicknesses of the soul. There it was, under the letter P: "PALINGENESIS: a method of breathing that allows you to achieve greater self-awareness and express repressed emotions. See also Rebirth."

There had been a renaissance, an evolution too, and they had generated fools. So Gabrielle Perron was tempted to think, fascinated as she was by the dust motes dancing in her library in the lamplight, despite that morning's dusting.

She pulled herself together, reminding herself that she hadn't settled in parallel with the world in order to detest it. She turned on her computer, created a file called GL under "Correspondence," and started a letter to the man who had been her first intellectual model and, all things considered, the only one.

Georges,

During a recent trip to Paris, I was tempted to see you again. To tell the truth it was a rash idea that struck me when I was crossing the Île de la Cité in a drizzle. I opened my umbrella just in front of your door, at 1 rue des Deux Ponts, and it took me a moment to realize that I was actually on the threshold of the building where I'd gone so often, with so many friends, part of the traffic that so exasperated your neighbours on every floor. The concierge who gave us a motherly greeting had flown away, were we not also half-plucked fledglings, far from our native lands, begging for the beakful of words from the assured talker that you are? Number 1 rue des Deux Ponts is now a blind door, soundly bolted, where the concierge is an electronic keypad displaying the apartment numbers. Caution or fear is so extreme that no name appears next to the numbers and I suppose that the entry code is changed every month, one must be prepared for the baseness of tradesmen.

That is so unlike you that I thought you'd retired to some North African land, surrounded still and again by those slender coffee-coloured lads you used to pretend to educate along with us, knowing we weren't taken in. As for me, I was quite fond of them, they added to my feeling of liberation, to the stirring sense that I'd finally reached a shore where everything was possible. I went into the bistro across the street, consulted a Paris directory and found you at the same address, immutable. I dialled the number once, twice, in vain. It was around six p.m., I decided to wait for you for a while, sitting at a table like a character in a Paris film, but over the course of an hour the only person I saw go inside was a little old lady who I'd have sworn, on account of her hard-wearing World War II–vintage raincoat, was the whining widow of the past, the one who shared your landing and murmured the worst racist remarks about your little North African friends. Her or her daughter. There's nearly a quarter century between me and that image, which I enjoyed rescuing from oblivion. But of Georges, nothing. Not on the following days either, when I dialled the number several times before giving up for good.

What did I want from you? When I was in Paris, nothing. I'd probably have hidden the fact that I was a cabinet minister, embarrassing in view of the values you'd inculcated in me, which were rather foreign to any exercise of power. Today though, Georges, I would ask you for an accounting of my life. I am now the age that you were, or nearly, when I first knew you. You were a creature of farandoles and words. What did the nature of your love affairs matter, your eyes were sated and bright in the morning and that, it seems to me, gave you even more words for picking away at our theses, for teaching us to recognize and describe "social change" as we said reverently at the time, that end in itself which you maintained had to be provoked before it could be analyzed. To bring about that change, you were offensive. We wanted to be. Your way of sating yourself with your little North African boys may have done more than all your books to give them access to knowledge, in the universities that were springing up in the suburbs. I came home from Europe telling myself that I too was going to have it all, farandoles and words and the social change that would come of it.

So what am I doing here, before I have one real wrinkle, organizing life as if it should no longer be touched?

I am still delighted, Georges, by what I, like you, contributed to breaking down. I hate what the world was before we got there, a bundle of fear and suffering dictated to the ignorant. I taught and taught, as a number of us did, and they came in the thousands to listen to us and to hand in their papers, as we'd done with you. But do you not also hear, in your educated and changed city, the sound of a new trivialization? Palingenesis has become "rebirth," Georges, and it's as if I were seeing you tonight, absent from 1 rue des Deux Ponts because you are giving adult paying students a course in the management of desire. Who knows, maybe you're even there, behind your electronic padlock?

And there's worse. I know of no one, absolutely no one, who has made a success of his farandole, the one that you promised us, that you said was the guaranteed companion of our knowledge.

I don't even know how to have a failed love affair. Yet if I take a good look, I have one. I'm one of those who have met a living being and then been inhabited by him, every second, and who have had the grace one day, in a train or in a car or in a strange bedroom, of hearing him say, "You've made a new man of me," while realizing he was happy at what he had become. And that's what loving is, and being loved. We didn't know how so much rapture could have come about. Bodies lived through it, there weren't enough sighs to steal from one another, enough salt to lick from the sphere of an eye or a small pink genital fold, of palms to press between legs before sleep, not too long, just before starting again, quickly. For the hours weigh double when they are parentheses stolen from other lives. And the love lasted, it still lasts, it is inexhaustible.

Except that it's no longer current. That living being no longer wants to say it or to enter my mouth or my belly. There were too many weeks between us, too long a road to travel in a few hours, we wasted the time that we needed to domesticate our worlds before we opened the sheets. We started to make love like others, who don't wait. We consummated, we consumed it. The weeks became months and now a year. He won't come back because we don't know how to be reborn. I ought to be tragic because he inhabits me still, every second. To such a point that it's he who kissed my neck or massaged my pubes when others clung to me and I smiled at them. I moved here to meet up with it, my failed love, a privilege that stemmed from it. But it makes light of me, breaking away and breaking my heart so thoroughly that I don't have one left to experience it.

And I'm angry with you, Georges, because I can look at us, at my love and me, I can observe every chink in our affair and dissect it, and understand it. Instead of inhabiting it, in this place that I wanted to be appropriate. It is you whom I hate tonight, because it was through you that the words came to me, sweeping over me today, driving away the ache. As a child, I used to speak the musical notes that way instead of listening to them. I believed you though when you explained that the right words were life itself and that what's more, we would have love. You were a crook. My wish for you, behind your bolted door, is a life of never-ending silence.

Through some inexplicable feeling of urgency, the letter was sent special delivery. On October 4, it came back to Gabrielle, stamped by the French post office, "Unknown at this address."

TWELVE

THE SHOW TO RAISE money for AIDS research took place amid chaos, or so the newspapers reported the next day, while the TV stations kept running footage of the small fire that had forced the evacuation of the maison de la culture around eleven p.m. The damage was limited; for some reason yet unknown one panel of the set had caught fire and, despite the swift arrival of firefighters, some parts of the set had been ruined. More than the fire itself, smoke and water damage would send the bill into the tens of thousands of dollars.

And so the fire had eclipsed the news stories that the team at the clinic had been so afraid of when a good dozen reporters and cameramen showed up in Laval just as the dignitaries were arriving, and clustered around some well-known faces. Including that of the minister of health, a decent man who had rejected the advice of his political attachés concerned about the disease's dissolute image. According to those who had skimmed the American press, which had more to say about this still mysterious subject, AIDS was not the terrible threat evoked by activists. It was indeed a devastating mortal ailment of a new kind, but it probably affected only the most debauched homosexuals, who were suddenly looking for pity. And even if they refused to pass moral judgement on the victims, it was still much too early to compromise themselves on the question of research assistance; they would seem to be rushing to meet that particular lobby while other foundations that battled terrible diseases were knocking at the ministry's door only to see their hopes constantly dashed. But the minister, because of some premonition about a greater disaster, had ignored their grimaces.

And so, along with Gabrielle and her colleague, Simon, he had been subjected to the questions that reporters borrowed from one another, few having taken the trouble to bone up on the thin file about the appearance of AIDS. Did the minister's presence indicate that the plague was a genuine epidemic, one that was beginning to spread through Quebec? That the situation was alarming? Were figures about deaths available? The answers were evasive and despite the PR people's pleas, the cameras ignored the young doctor, the sole respondent who could have given accurate information and calm the first signs of hysteria. With his slender adolescent's manner and his anonymous looks, he was left to the scientific press, absent from the show to which editors had chosen to assign general reporters. The worst had seemed about to happen when the lenses started scanning the small crowd gathered in the main lobby, a majority of long-haired males, a large proportion of whom sported an earring. It seemed as if the evening would be a model of the art of creating stereotypes, when the goal had been to create a breach in the wall of prejudices. An imminent disaster.

The fire then had been a wrong in exchange for a right because it had modified the structure of the news reports, eliminated idiotic questions about AIDS and even — something no newspaper would talk about — put an end to an embarrassing situation that had suddenly arisen on stage, just before the final speech.

The organizers had had a terrible time coming up with the lineup of performers. Given their casual ways, their extroverted temperaments, their well-known generosity and the boldness of the event, recruiting volunteers should have been easy. But nearly all the voices at the other end of the line turned vague. As if in the grip of some unspeakable terror. Idiotic excuses were stammered, conversations were abruptly broken off, leaving messages was pointless, everyone was much too busy this season. Except for Pauline Julien, who was always magnificently responsive to the call, the rare brave ones had materialized from the serious musical circles, notably contemporary music. In other words, celebrities no one had ever heard of, though they'd been the pride of Quebec in the international networks of the avant-garde. And so, even by extending her dissonant repertoire to include some Mahler lieder that the average mortal wouldn't find too unsettling, the sublimely talented soprano wouldn't make the ticket office blow up. As for the more popular groups or singers, whose melodies would definitely have been closer to the tastes of the young, male, gay audience, the best-known had dodged the invitation and they'd ended up with the B list of new talent that had not yet hit its stride. So that to fill the two hours of showtime, including the intermission, they'd had to resort to some postrural poets, a very productive but very private network, eagerly awaiting the rare opportunities to make their work known. Pauline, who had agreed not only to sing but also to host the evening, had promised to introduce them so warmly that the audience, even if it included a few backward individuals still loyal to formalist aesthetics, would willingly applaud poetry that was impossible to read and consequently to chant. The poets would be asked to offer nothing that would exceed the attention span of an average crowd, in other words, three minutes and change.

But that was without reckoning with Clothaire Lemelin. He it was who had begotten the postrural school of poetry and he fully intended to exercise his primogeniture. He had reserved the closing act for himself.

Dramatic in a charcoal suit and red tie, reminders of apocalypse, he perched on the edge of the platform, demanded total darkness onstage, save on his person, so as to highlight his mane of hair with its blue-tinged waves and his white, nearly diaphanous hands — the hands of a full-time visionary.

"What I am about to deliver was written and published in Paris, for close friends, a good many years ago. You'll see that it's an occasional poem. But as its style will attest, it is neither by me nor by our friends here present. It was written by a gentleman who passed away last night, at Montreal's Sacré-Coeur Hospital, of natural causes, that is they had nothing to do with AIDS. That death, however, coming on the eve of your gathering, must be brought to your attention because it sheds light on those deaths that we are recalling here and another death, on the same order, that Quebec is striving towards, its current negligence announcing the death pangs."

A murmur of impatience ran through the thin ranks of VIPs. They had been assured of an apolitical show, an order Pauline Julien had scrupulously respected. Was this a trap? The zealot inhaled their concern, looked up to the flies and began to declaim from memory his chosen piece.

> In the dead of night, embittered and alone,
> I set down lines unfit to be read by man.
> I am a pilgrim who has clambered far too high,
> Beyond pleasure for the hand or for the eye.
> My mad shunning of this sordid world
> Augments with age and implacable distaste;
> I can but oppose a passive face
> To monsters brought to life by some fiend's rage.
> I thrust my icy scalpel into nature's breast,

And sound the boundless baseness of the flesh.
Whoever would prevail against this rot
Must bow before the connoisseurs of hell,
A hell that's of this world and observes no truce.
Pilgrim of the infinite, votary of the beyond,
Why seek in other climes what you desire
When you may sink with ease into this mire?

"Your stomach turns of course," continued Clothaire
Lemelin, "when you hear that accumulation of dripping
alexandrines, detrimental to the memory of Baudelaire who
has never been so poorly imitated. Pretentious too, thinking
he's an albatross shot down by the rest of us, the carrion universe. There's worse. I only recited a poem suited to the
occasion, one that talks about flesh and death. But that poet
had something for every taste, from Claudel to Nelligan, idiotic images, moon-women who were also flaming suns,
books that rhymed with crooks, and even inane advice to
the lovelorn.

I withdraw into myself
And find myself serene
More enduring than tears in their dotage
Life is a joyful pilgrimage.

"Composing such trivia, it would have been better had
he died sooner. Yet this versifier, writing a century after the
genuine writers of melancholy, was one of the greatest intellectual influences in French Canada, one of the first literary
figures to recognize the foundations of the independence
movement, as well as being the symbol of our collective
apostasy, for he gave up the soutane long before those noisily
defrocked priests turned sexologists. He deserved praise,

François Hertel, about whom you'll read hagiographies in the papers tomorrow, whose coffin certain eminent federalists will follow because he taught them how to read, he gave absolution to their first ejaculations — alone or in company — and he had the good sense to choose exile before he began to express his doubts about Canada. Tonight, I am presenting him to you as he was and as we are. Phony tragedians, borrowed fanatics, about to be chilled forever."

Then Clothaire Lemelin, who now was pacing the stage under a follow spot, the lighting man thinking he was obliged to use it, launched into a disjointed but not uninteresting soliloquy, talking in particular about the end of innocence.

During that year, 1985, the irruption of AIDS into public awareness had driven us from the brief paradise of a decade of debauchery that had been a genuine freedom, one that others would envy us for until the end of time. For of that serene, intense copulation had emerged, thanks to the sacred still clinging to us, loving passions of biblical quality, the most genuine since the world began.

That night however we said together the *Ite Missa Est* which it was agreed had been uttered by Hertel, the former Jesuit. His death in that year, 1985, marked the end of the intellectual dilettantism that had allowed an entire generation to listen to itself talk about the country with a felicitous candour that its descendants would envy, like its moral freedom, forever. From that demented, Hertelian, boundless chattering had been born in some of our hearts a revolt so powerful that the country had been lived before it came into being. This wouldn't happen again. The advent of AIDS, after the lost referendum, brought us into an era of precautions. To preserve what remnant of life?

Clothaire Lemelin, battered by the depressing prospects

he evoked, was losing his vehemence, carefully picking his words, stretching out some silences that even Pauline couldn't interrupt to bring it to a conclusion. The entire house was impatient now, having opted out of this grim discourse that had far exceeded the three minutes prescribed. The health minister, brave as ever, was getting ready to simply go onstage; he would walk briskly, shake hands with Lemelin while murmuring admiration of the poet's presentation, and the follow spot would abandon the nervous man. The closing speech would come back to the main question — the need to mobilize around AIDS research. As for sovereignty, the minister was one of those who thought it was dormant, bound to come back, people mustn't worry about it the way those poets do, they tend to exaggerate. It was enough for a two-minute address.

Clothaire had launched into a roundabout speech on the inevitable massacre of the innocent when a slight commotion shook the wings. Flames were already licking out on the left, at the screen where the video was projected in a loop. The first thing to burn was the portrait of François Dubeau.

There was no panic — with its wide corridors and numerous exits the auditorium was easy to evacuate. The small crowd had time to congratulate itself some more outside while the firemen did their work. In general, people were laughing at Clothaire Lemelin.

With a shrill voice, his chest bulging in an expensive leather jacket, a clean, well-groomed young man was dominating a conversation with others like him at the entrance to the parking lot. He was lashing out at the organizers of the evening. A retrograde idea, in his opinion, to have accepted, even solicited, the presence of Lemelin and his disciples. "No wonder we lost the referendum, when we give the floor to a bunch of incompetents who've served their time, who ought to go home and cultivate their pot and smoke it before they go to sleep in their beds after spending the day asleep on their feet. It's because of them that we're blocked, I've been waiting eight years for a permanent job teaching literature at a CEGEP in the Laurentians where the students are bored to death by their pathetic bullshit. Did you hear that lecture of his on the symbolism of the death of François Hertel? Tomorrow he'll waste the time of his stunned students who are suffering through their first literature courses, unloading this totally uninteresting story, those pedantic musings on a minor player who's just gone to join Adjutor Rivard in the limbo of our literature. Clothaire Lemelin doesn't even have a doctorate, he has no scientific apparatus, they're all phonies, he and his followers. They already were when they were teaching me because I had the bad luck of being in the first generation of CEGEP students. One day we got stuck with some semiological ineptitude to justify the triteness of their poems, the next day it was digressions on the liberation of Quebec, and the day after that, if the weather was grey, their perorations on the absurd, topped off with their feigned melancholy à la Marguerite Duras. No consistency, no structure to their thinking. And besides, they weren't very clean, they had bad breath, never changed their shirts, smoked Gitanes . . ."

This speech had an undeniable success. A girl, the only one in the group, with arms crossed and eyes bright, took up the crusade. "And those dimwits are selling this evening short. What they should have done to benefit AIDS research was organize a prestigious public lecture, invite Professor Montanier, get interviews in all the media, examine the scientific angle instead of constantly falling back on music. As if we haven't moved beyond old folk songs. They're provincials totally out of touch with what's going on in the world and all they can do is gripe. They're a disgrace."

Gabrielle, slightly off to the side, picked up only bits of what the woman said, distracted as she was by the appearance of Pierre, with whom she'd expected to go back to rue des Bouleaux. The little group's bitterness upset her. She was quite fond of Clothaire Lemelin, whom she'd run into at various forums, even if he nearly always disputed the cultural policies of her government, of all governments. She envied him his easy indignation and she'd probably kept in some box of files the wonderful letter he'd sent her, in an official but luminous tone, to threaten the State with the collective resignation of all its poets if the project of liberating Quebec were put on the back burner: "Madame Minister, we will no longer be the carriers of your stars if you become the sawyers of our dreams . . ."

True, there was no follow-up to the letter, literary circles were much too divided. And above all, if a collective resignation by the poets were to be taken seriously, they'd have had to turn their backs on programs that provided grants to artists, programs that, though modest, were much sought after by the poets in the CEGEPs who unlike their university colleagues didn't have access to sabbatical leaves, but would also like to spend some time writing in Provence. The missive had remained a secret between her and Clothaire. She had kindly invited him to lunch at a bistro in the Petit-Champlain neighbourhood and it consoled him over his friends' desertion, he wanted to repudiate them. As a sociologist, she had put forward some objective findings on human nature, on the prevalence of mediocrity save during periods of severe crisis. It was obvious that Quebec wasn't experiencing one, or at least didn't think that it was. They took time to sip a cognac after coffee, something that hadn't been done since the sixties. The small group that was gravitating tonight around the junior lecturer with a Ph.D in literature most likely didn't know the taste, just as the young woman with a scientific heart most likely no longer swallowed semen and possibly never had. It was the age of white wine and, increasingly, the condom.

Gabrielle returned to the building, there was only one fire engine at the rear entrance, the hoses were being rolled up. In the lobby she spotted Pierre in conversation with two police officers, the female one was taking notes. She went up to them, it was over now, and she realized vaguely that Pierre had had something to do with starting the fire but that, until further notice, the matter was being treated as an accident. He had left a dry rag on a turned-off spotlight, the lighting man had switched it on again to follow Clothaire, the rag had caught fire and the screen upstage a few centimetres away had burst into flames. He would be questioned again tomorrow should the need arise, but that was enough for tonight. Anyway, there were no other witnesses.

Gabrielle wasn't sure what to think. The story held together, it was hard to imagine anything that would have driven him to wreak havoc, but he seemed to her to have the evil eye. He appeared to find it natural to walk home with her in the cool clear night, beneath a froth of milky clouds.

They walked past vacant lots, bungalows, cottages, a small shopping centre with all its lights off, the jumble of remnants of what had been thirty years earlier a village and its surrounding countryside. The night lent charm to the disparate neighbourhood, it seemed possible that children lived out their secrets there, that the forsaken lived torrid affairs with individuals come from foreign parts, that cuckolded husbands would rather pamper their cars than defy intruders, and that the streets enjoyed recounting it from one celebration to the next. And that a boy who was fated to be a writer would one day turn it into a multivolume best-seller, gem of Quebec literature.

Pierre became serene once more. Again he described the fire, showed himself to be concerned about the damage but not really sorry. She shared his lightness, what could one do, these things happen. Then came the question, which he asked in a casual tone: "Did you know that guy François Dubeau, the one with the picture up on the screen that burned?" She paid no attention to his peculiar curiosity, he shouldn't have even known François Dubeau's name, he was just a teenager with time on his hands, poorly educated, conscripted into doing odd jobs. "I knew him slightly. He was a great art critic, at least he was very respected here in Quebec. But he stayed in his own world, the university, peri-odicals, symposiums, away from the political battles, very different from someone like Clothaire Lemelin, for instance. All I know is that he was very influential and that his death was a shock in his milieu."

Pierre kept trying, despite her vague answers. "And how could he have died of AIDS?" Gabrielle started. "He was homosexual, you know, he was even considered to be particularly active, his travels, the baths, all that . . . He was one of the first to be struck by the virus, it's because of him that the others started becoming a little more aware of the danger . . ."

Pierre stopped, grabbed her elbow to slow her down, became abrupt. "That doesn't make sense, what you're say-ing. I knew him, he was Marie's boyfriend, he slept with her, he was at the house a lot. I know I'm right, his name was François, it was him."

Gabrielle sighed. "Are you sure? Lots of intellectuals resemble one another. Still, it's possible. In those circles you see all sorts of things. All I can tell you is that he certainly didn't have a reputation for being interested in women."

Why was it so important to him to stir up that old story? François Dubeau was dead. Marie was dead. And if she had been his lover, she had well and truly survived him for a while, she too had moved to Laval, made a new life for herself, a job. There was no connection between their deaths. A few minutes from rue des Bouleaux, Gabrielle tried to inculcate in Pierre, in the simplest words, some notion of the dissociation between human beings and their sexual practices, a phenomenon now prevalent, for better or worse. To please him, or so she thought, she brought up the possibility of a genuine love between François and Marie, despite François's other affairs. Maybe he couldn't afford to be seen with a woman: his sexual practices were part of his image. Social prohibitions, she explained laboriously, always find a way to renew themselves. And then she reminded him — because she had to conclude her remarks, they'd reached the freshly turned earth of the begonia bed — who were they to judge?

She heard her own emancipated tone, she recognized the inner voice that had authorized her also to be unfaithful to whomever she wanted. "Really, Pierre, we can't judge."

It would not have been surprising, after that lecture on animal nature, for him to try to end the night between Gabrielle's sheets. But he made no such move. They took the elevator in his stubborn silence. Just as the doors were opening he held them for a moment. "I'm leaving the apartment for good three days from now. I'll drop in tomorrow night if you want and show you some of Marie's papers." Why not? Gabrielle was filled with curiosity. That's what happens when you become a well-behaved woman, she thought before falling asleep, easily, sated with the good suburban air, naked but with no appetite. Short news items can be interesting.

THIRTEEN

AND SO, ON THE MORNING of October 6, 1985, Gabrielle Perron embarked upon another new life, with the exhilaration that accompanies such resolutions. Her retreat to 10,005 rue des Bouleaux, as she had finally realized, had been until then a simple flight, as several of her acquaintances muttered. Next stop suicide, she upbraided herself as she emerged from the perfectly streaming shower, inhaling the tender scent of the creams that though not perfumed, give women of every age the illusion that they are pleasant to the touch. But death has no appeal for her. None.

A sound mind in a sound body, she took a rapid count of the disappointments she'd been turning over in her mind since her return in the spring. The sum was large. Lost love, of which she had sullied the memory by succumbing to others. Lost country, for which she had been one of the first to give up hope. Lost ideas, of which she had cut ties with her former master. Lost beings, for she hadn't been able to give them her time — which was lost as well.

The inmost depths should have sucked her in, she saw that very clearly through the finest black coffee. But vertigo didn't come. Her life had been anything but a tragedy, of that she was well aware. Even if she were gnawed at by a cancer, she thought, she'd have had no reason to complain. She could simply go out and listen to the murmur of the city to discover some real calamities. She'd met so many: women terrified by their children's mental handicaps, fathers hopeless because they couldn't make ends meet, ugly girls walled up inside rejection, drudges weighed down by contempt, old women collapsed at the backs of buses or on park benches.

And the cripple at the university, remember him, Gabrielle, that superior intellect imprisoned within dribbling speech, whom you all avoided in company? He was there last night, at the AIDS benefit, taking in the sobs of the beautiful people over a disease of the beautiful people.

The unhappiness of those like Gabrielle was merely a facsimile. Despite multiple impasses, it had to be pushed away like a guilty thought. Today would be the day for her to do what was necessary to ship it away towards exterior darkness, the day when the confinement she'd chosen would take on its meaning, when she would stop doing things by halves. She smiled, was amused to think of herself as the reincarnation of Jeanne Le Ber, the recluse of Nouvelle-France, walled inside her father's house of her own free will and surviving on bread and water, for the redemption of the nonbelievers. That story had made a big impression on her at school, not so much for its salutary merits as for the logistical problems it posed. How did she wash? Who dealt with the chamber pots? Who cut her hair? The nuns didn't talk about such things and no pupil would have dared to ask, so the image of Jeanne Le Ber remained duly virginal. No, Gabrielle preferred to see herself as Laure Clouet, her story taken up again long after its conclusion, when the old maid from the Grande Allée, whom readers had seen straightening her shoulders and soaking up the sensual sun in the final pages of Adrienne Choquette's novel, would many years later approach the other shore of her liberation. Tall and still beautiful, well-educated about men's bodies and maybe about women's too, having had a glimpse of what Quebec could have been, had it wanted, she would be neither weary nor bitter but determined to remove herself from the tumult, to seize from inside everything that the intense outside had brought her. She would go back inside her beautiful house, quietly close the door and make of it an appropriate place for her detachment.

The spirit of the cloister was turning up here. At its best, though, that is without the absurdity of renunciation. No servitude towards God and his saints, no sacrifice of the earthly nourishment that we discover so much more effectively after forty, generally imported, like fine wines and exquisite woollens. "All human evil," Pascal had decreed, "comes from this, man's being unable to sit still in a room." Recalling that lovely cliché, Gabrielle saw it as a challenge over which she could triumph. She experienced a conceit similar to what she felt after her first successful speeches, proof that no nun was asleep in her.

On the first detachable page in one of the large-size Rhodia writing pads she'd accumulated with the idea that one day she would write important things in them, she listed the prerequisites for her new life:

- to look at every document she'd brought from her Quebec City office and get rid of whatever should not be turned over to the National Archives;
- to renounce officially and permanently any sexual adventure that was not a loving relationship (and therefore, no doubt, give them up for good);
- in the proper time and place, to recall the splendour of the lover's touch and manage to experience it again;
- to undertake to read the finest works available to humankind, limiting herself however to works of fiction, which tell of history and humans so much better;
- to acquire a cat, a young one so that its life expectancy can match hers.

The list was odd, but perfectible. She saw it as a good start, some ways to relegate the past without denying it and an entry, through books and the cat, into a welcoming room. She had just succumbed to the notion of a cat after having long rejected it. She liked cats, from little grey-and-white balls of fluff to fat yellow crippled alley cats, but she hated the old-maid appearance they give to the women who pamper them, talk to them, turn them into presences. Another attitude to reappraise. And she'd do it that very day, inviting Madeleine to lunch at Vito's, for old times' sake, then taking her along as a consultant to the SPCA, the ideal spot to find a gutter kitten, the toughest species and the smartest, as hers was duty bound to be.

Côte-des-Neiges was teeming with students still in the daze that marked the beginning of the school year, you could see them in groups at bookstores, drugstores, hardware stores, stocking up for the next academic year which most would have tired of by February, when the neighbourhood would close in around its frozen mud and its poorly maintained apartment blocks. Few went to Vito's, the restaurant now attracting mostly professors or retired people from the neighbourhood, for the prices had gone up though the food was still the same, Italo-Québécois for stomachs equally hybridized. The owner counted on nostalgia, which helped him hold on to his past clientele, now sufficiently well-heeled that they no longer drank house wine by the litre. He chose well, Gabrielle and Madeleine had trouble finding a table in the first room, facing the street. The former minister, still recognizable, attracted looks, and she regretted her unthinking choice of restaurant, this was no way to start a new life, being stuck here in the territory of gossip for which she provided an excellent pretext. They were reduced to whispering rather than speaking out loud and Madeleine, who wanted to talk Gabrielle out of her desire for a cat, couldn't complete her arguments. She would have ridiculed, caricatured her friend, got carried away a little, but she limited herself to pointing out the problems of maintenance — litter, food, smells — and care. "And most of all, don't count on me!" "I won't need a cat sitter." Gabrielle displayed an ethereal smile which displeased her friend intensely and brought their discussion to an end.

Definitely, this was a difficult turning point in a woman's life, thought Madeleine, who for some time now had been rather concerned about her own capacity for enjoyment. It wasn't a symptom of menopause, hormones erased them easily, but a lessening of her appetite for fun. She who had never sought brainy partners found herself too often, once her legs were together again, regretting that they had nothing to say. Besides that, she was reading a little more; soon she too would be contemplating a cat.

On rue Jean-Talon they were warmly welcomed at the SPCA, where the July dispersal of pussycats left behind when their masters had moved was not yet over. The choice was quickly made: an animal just a few months old, housebroken and having had all its shots, that displayed even in its golden eyes the self-confidence of the big tabby cat it would become, introverted but likable, and adaptable to a cloistered life. The young woman who dealt with adoption procedures had no idea who Gabrielle Perron was and observed the rule of suspicion to the letter. Gabrielle had to answer questions about the lifestyle in store for the cat as well as about her own abilities, psychological and financial, to devote the necessary time to its happiness and health. Finally, the cat was in a box on the backseat, dignified and silent like the good companion it would be.

"What will you call him?"

"Hertel."

Madeleine, who got her news from television only and therefore knew nothing about Hertel's death, wondered if her friend was heading for a breakdown. She promised herself to call her more often. For now though she was in a hurry, she had a tennis lesson before dinner.

She just had time to buy all sorts of cat things at a pet store before it closed and Gabrielle was finally at home. While she was getting to know Hertel, she renewed the determination that had been given a rough ride by her stop at Vito's. After a shower, she donned a royal blue dressing gown, its velvet like warm silk, and remembered, as she put in the oven a vegetarian lasagne precooked at a steep price, that Pierre was probably going to turn up. He bothered her, that was another of today's mistakes, fortunately the last one because he was leaving soon. She was about to change again because it was out of the question to greet him dressed like this, when he rang the bell. Too bad, she'd simply cut the meeting short, she certainly wouldn't invite him to share her dinner.

In fact he was the one who said he couldn't stay long. She had no reason to worry about how she was dressed, he didn't look at her. He handed her Marie's notebook, the one that the federal government had given him once the formalities were complete and they couldn't track down other family or friends. The notebook confirmed Marie's relationship with François Dubeau, she had to read it, and there were references to Gabrielle too. They settled in, face to face, in the library. Her first truly solitary evening was in ruins.

The pages had been read and reread, skimming through them she had the impression that the boy was following the progress of her reading. But eventually she forgot that he was there. She absorbed Marie's words as if the notebook were a testament intended for her; she saw the woman at her side, slender, brunette, dressed in red, delivering her story aloud, line by line. Exorcism would drive away the Cain who was spoiling the moment and the two women would stay behind to share, until late at night and maybe till the next day and after, reproaches to the wicked gods who had caused them to be born in the wrong places. Most important, they would have shared their way of leaving them. Marie urgently, Gabrielle calmly. After all, they were both barren, and free.

She smiled at her interior movie with its triumphal ending and turned towards Pierre. She wished he could leave the notebook with her until he left, there were passages in it to be copied out and kept, in the past she'd have urged publication. "What a pity, that accident," she said, "she was so right to go away . . ." He folded his arms and straightened his shoulders as if he had become a man. "Do you think so?"

She was too distracted by her vision of Marie to pay attention to the hostile crackle of the question. She was about to speak, to serve up to this boy, who was on the whole rather uncouth, some cliché in praise of flight, when he cut her off, suddenly standing, shouting because he'd never really learned how to talk. "It was me that started the fire yesterday. I've been doing that since I was born. I'm unhappy. I don't understand anything. You always lie. And when you're tired of telling lies you put on airs, you talk about exile. What's that supposed to mean, exile? Do you know what it means for me? I started the fire while that crazy poet was talking about it. Marie died in exile. And it's your fault, you and people like you. You can read in the notebook, a country of the destroyed. She went away. She was mine since the day I was born. And you say she was right . . ."

He grabbed the notebook from her, rested his elbows on her art books, a rather fine collection from the primitive artists of Oceania to the conceptual artists of Europe. At his fingertips, Marie's pages began to blaze. Where had the lighter come from? In Gabrielle's eyes there was none.

If the victim had not been till recently the minister of cultural affairs, the crime on rue des Bouleaux would have been in the headlines for a day at most, and even then on an inside page. It was a classic story, barely juicy: a forty-year-old woman stabbed, an awkward attempt to camouflage the murder with a quickly extinguished fire in an apartment building equipped with every alarm and fire-prevention device, the young occupant of a neighbouring apartment being held for questioning and then jailed on convincing evidence, no other witnesses, especially since the building had been without a concierge for several weeks. Emotions were guarded on this street in a new section of Laval where, despite her brief career in politics, the woman was one more unknown among others. All the same, some concerns were expressed about peace and quiet in the neighbourhood. Had it not been for the detail of the cat acquired on the very day of the tragedy and sent back at once to the SPCA, orphaned again, the dose of pathos would have been nil.

In spite of orders to be discreet, the police still had to deal with a certain commotion, and the story had spilled over from the pages devoted to news in brief and seeped into the political coverage, where the right to comment made possible some fanciful exaggerations. One declared that a colleague of Gabrielle Perron's claimed her seclusion resulted from a depression of amorous origin, another took up the depression theory the next day but attributed it to the blocking of the sovereignist horizon, because she belonged to the idealistic side of the party. Another, more audacious, focussed on the crime itself, suggesting that the official trail of the investigation, attempted robbery, was an indulgent official cover-up for a sex scandal, Gabrielle Perron's life having long seemed, let us say, unorthodox. Whatever the truth may have been, it was a very sad ending for a talented woman whose retirement had already been seen as political suicide.

The sole female editorial writer at *Le Devoir*, who was the same age as Gabrielle and had always found it interesting to run into her, contributed a brief but heartfelt piece marked by sympathy for the life of a recluse. "In the space known as Quebec, where for a quarter of a century now our generation has never stopped ceding its overly vivid hopes to the lasting practitioners of the old forms of resignation, interior exile freely chosen is an act of courage." Nothing about the circumstances of the death, they were of secondary importance, an editorial must try to take the readers' thoughts a little further.

And that was the tomb of Gabrielle Perron, made of paper henceforth recyclable. As for the apartment she had owned, a buyer was found quickly. A securities broker, recently divorced, assured of the speculative potential of a good location along the river, moved in with a new girlfriend, to an appropriate place.